I0518672

Shusuke's Dream

Can you change the world?

~The Origin of Wagyu Beef~

Yoshiko Kagawa

Copyright © 2023
Yoshiko Kagawa

Shusuke's Dream
Can you change the world?

Translator: Kiemi Shibata
Chief Editor: Lloyd Peace
Coordinator: Junko Rodriguez

Published by Babel Press U.S.A.
All rights reserved

ISBN: 978-1-7377083-1-5

Babel Corporation
1833 Kalakaua Avenue, Suite 208,
Honolulu, Hawaii 96815, US

Table of Contents

Chapter 1

Dawn at Ojiro Village

As if to divide the layers of mountains, silky veil-like clouds are absolute still, seen dimly in the darkness.

The orange light from the sun leaks out through the slit between the sea of clouds and the horizon, peeking at the world beneath, and then precipitously, the light turns into silver and dashes horizontally all at once. Instantly, the floating silky veils are colored lilac.

Then, the tiny sun emerging from the valley pushes away the lilac-colored sea of clouds. In no time, lilac veils become thinner and thinner, as if they were being drawn into a different dimension. Now, the world on the earth begins revealing its shape. When the entire area is surrounded by the gradually shifting colors, from the purple sky, then orange, yellow, and white ground on the bottom, morning finally arrives here in Ojiro.

The hazy and chilly air remains on earth. There, I could see a herd of black cows grazing. Bathing under the morning sun, their backs seem to be covered in fine indigo velvet. Their relaxed movements make me realize that this easy tempo and image may embody a peaceful life.

Before I know it, Mozart's Clarinet Concerto No. 2 is playing in my mind, which always causes tears to roll down my cheeks. I'm not sure if this is called sentimentality or not, but anyway, I feel gratitude for the fact that I am alive and for nature's activities.

I wonder how many times I've been here to see this scenery......

Whenever I feel gloomy or need to lift my spirits, I like to come here from Marseille to visit.

My hometown was set on endless rolling hills while this countryside village perches on the slopes of a small valley surrounded by impassable mountains. This view is not quite the same as my hometown, yet for some reason, it reminds me of my home.

When I was young, I used to work as a French cook. But life is a strange thing. It only took one person and one movie to turn my destiny 180 degrees around, and now I am teaching (sort of) political philosophy to many college students.

What I want my students to grasp from learning political philosophy is that "each individual has all the answers to find the right passage of life." Simply, having them realize it is my job. Surprisingly, it comes naturally to me, and I find it much more interesting than cooking. Considering my cooking skills, it won't be so difficult to replace me as a chef, but I believe that this job is an important mission exclusively for me to utilize my unique sense to fulfill what it takes.

Yes ...... I think this is the answer to what I should do in my life.

Today, I arrived in Japan to give a university extension lecture to international students. Well, I'd better get going now......

Chapter 2

Public Lecture

When I arrived at the lecture room at the university, TV crews had just started setting up for the live TV broadcast. A female guide was kindly leading me to the professors' waiting room, but I chose to decline. Observing people doing their work was much more entertaining, so I stayed out of the way to watch how they prepared. Everyone, including the producer, cameraman, and even an anchor as well, was helping each other and working enthusiastically together to achieve one purpose. It was a delightful sight. In a way, my ideal "peace" seemed to be realized there, right at that moment. I was deep in such thoughts when the director called and pulled me back to reality.

"Mr. Francoise, please stand by. A hundred twenty seconds after the music starts, I will raise my left hand to signal you. Then, you will come out from the right side and walk up to the stage."

I hurried to the classroom entrance. Soon, many students rushed into the classroom through the back door. About two hundred seats in this classroom were filled with various ethnicities in the blink of an eye.

"Stand by.......Get set...Go!"

With the director's single word, everyone was on pins and needles. The music started. It was "Jounetsu Tairiku" by Taro Hakase. That unexpectedly up-tempo number made me feel a little awkward, so I grinned. Then, the large screen set in front of the stage displayed, "International Lecture by Professor Francoise. 'Can you make the world a better place?'"

The beautiful anchor lady with fair skin in a fitted blue knit dress began to speak facing camera one.

"Today, we have many students from various countries all over the world. They are international exchange students invited to the Toukei University of Japan for a public lecture by Professor Francoise. Produced by FVT, and I, Nancy Goldsmith, am MC and...."

"Also, I'm her assistant, Hiroyuki Watanabe. Professor Francoise specially prepared a video for today. This is such a wonderful opportunity. All right then, let me introduce, Professor Andre Francoise from the University of Lyon."

The director raised his left hand. As I was entering the classroom through the right front entrance, a loud round of applause welcomed me. Feeling excited, I raised my hand to greet the audience and quickly went up onto the stage. With my right arm resting on the table, I began talking with a rush of emotion. That's how I always stand while giving lectures.

"First, I want to ask you folks a question. Raise your hand if you believe that you can make this world better in the future."

Students hesitantly look at each other before some started to slowly raise their hands. I was a little stunned since more students raised their hands than I had expected. I tried to count them with my fingers, but I gave up halfway and waved my hand side-to-side.

"Wow, uncountable. I'm quite impressed. I appreciate your bravery. Okay, then, what about you? The third row from the front, in the yellow sweater with black-framed glasses. Could you stand up for me please?"

Taken by surprise, he pointed at himself and looked around uncertainly.

"Yes, you. What is your name?"

Since he did not even raise his hand yet was chosen unexpectedly, he seemed not too excited about this role. His slim body was half squatting so I couldn`t tell if he was standing up or not, but eventually, he stood up straight. He must be Japanese without a doubt. From the appearance, it is hard to tell the difference between Japanese, Koreans, and Chinese, but Koreans and Chinese have more confidence in themselves and speak without hesitation in this type of situation.

"....... I'm Ken......, Ken Tanaka."

"Hi, Ken. Ken, you didn't raise your hand, did you? Why do you think you cannot make the world a better place?"

I was trying to ask casually. But he seemed to be embarrassed, looking down and fixing his glasses a bit more than necessary.

"Well....um..., I am still learning a lot of things, so...um... it's not yet clear to me what I am interested in or what I would like to do, not so particular. Let alone, I have never thought of what I can do for the world. My current concern is to come to school and pass exams. That's all I am concerned about now."

"Okay, thank you. Everyone, give him applause."

He seemed to be surprised by the generous applause from the audience, lifted his chin, and looked around.

"You are such an honest person, Ken. Actually, I believe that's what the majority of people would think. Grown-ups are also too busy living their own lives to take a moment to think of others. Even so, I don't think you believe this world is a perfect place and has no problems that need to be addressed, don't you agree?"

"Well, yes. I am aware of some problems like the ultra-extremist organizations, potential threats from our neighboring countries, or the declining population of Japan. But there is not much I can do about those problems. After all, I am only a bystander...."

"I see. Then, how about in the future, after you study hard and gain much more experience and skills?"

"I don't think I have such potential. While my friends enthusiastically volunteered after the great earthquake, I, ...honestly, didn't feel like doing that. I would be quite satisfied with an average life with an average family and becoming a common worker who goes to a bar after a long day of hard work."

I was glad to hear his straightforward answer, which I did not expect him to share. This is the real voice of a real student.

"I see. It is, indeed, what many people may think of themselves, too. Thank you for bravely sharing your honest thoughts. Well then, I would like to hear opposing opinions. How about you, the young lady sitting on the third from the left? You raised your hand, didn't you?"

"Yes. I'm Anita. I am an exchange student from Nairobi, majoring in science."

I nodded deeply at her regal demeanor.

"So, Anita, you raised your hand to my question, thinking that you can change the world to a better place. Could you explain to me why you think so?"

The third camera quickly captured her face, panning from the side.

"We, minorities, have a history of victimized slavery. About fifty years ago, Martin Luther King Jr. made his famous speech, 'I have a dream, that one day on the red hills of Georgia, the sons of former slaves and the sons of former slave owners will be able to sit down together at the table of brotherhood.'

Back then, our ancestors who were labeled as slaves could not possibly come up with such a dream. However, once his dream was transformed into words in front of the audience, the dream of a person who had a strong faith in what he believed became our shared dream. Soon after, people were convinced that it would become true in the future. And now, I am standing here happily. No one would accuse me even though I am now sitting at a desk with people from all over the world. So, I believe that I can change the world one day if I am truly aware of the issues, have a dream to resolve them, and dare to act. Just one person's opinion creates a tiny ripple, which will eventually grow into a whirlpool involving everyone. With that, at least it moves the world in the right direction."

The audience gave her a standing ovation, and a nearby student hugged Anita's shoulder expressing how moving her opinion was. I couldn't help but be moved as well. The first camera was eager to capture Anita and her surroundings from the front angle, so, fortunately, the elation on my face was not broadcasted on TV.....

"Does anyone disagree with Anita? She said that strong awareness of the issue will change the world. With that said, even if you are aware of the issue but have no strong faith, then it's just a mere picture. Ken, don't you think so? But let's not pick on him for not taking any action because most of us just draw mere pictures of our dream without realizing it. Now, Ken mentioned the ultra-extremist organizations earlier. Do you think there is something we can do to change that, too? I assume we are all aware of this issue, aren't we?"

Everyone was looking around not raising their hands. A moment later, a male student hesitantly lifted his hand halfway up.

"Great, please stand up."

Surprised, the audience looked at the Caucasian man.

"I'm Gary Nicol, and I'm from the United States. I believe that ultra-extremist organizations can be changed for the better, or rather, must be changed for their sake.

I used to be a full-time worker once. So, I might be a little older than everyone else here. When I was trying to find a job, I got rejected by all the companies I wanted to work for. Even though I finally got a job, I kept making mistakes over and over. I was so disappointed with myself, which eventually led me to resign from the job. The president of the company did not even try to stop me. Looking back, I wasn't mature enough to think of my life more seriously.

I had no social status, no insurance, or food to eat. Volunteers would give me bread and soup, but those weren't what I sought. I wanted to find value in myself as a human being. But no one cared about me. Neither my father nor my mother did anything for me. But later, I realized that it was their way to greatly express their parental love.

My father owns a large company, so it would have been easy for him to reach out to me, but he chose to pretend not to see it. I felt like I was simply a pathetic, worthless loser who had been cast out of society. My misery turned to rage. I was paranoid enough to imagine that even those volunteers, to whom I should have been thankful, must have looked down on me as a young but helpless washout, who can do nothing, underneath their smiles. I was urged to do something, but nothing good came out of it.

Blaming others around me or politics was the only way for me to refrain from killing myself. I searched for and visited the extremists' websites over and over. "'Maybe, they will find the true value of me....... I will take revenge on this world. I will take revenge on everyone who rejected me. I am an honest and hard worker. How dare they rejected me! Gradually, such thoughts dominated my mind........ Then one day, I guess they knew that I visited their website often, extremists contacted me, inviting me to join their activities. It was the only good thing that happened to me. They were the only ones that accepted me as a person.

But my father found out that I was exchanging emails with them. In my dimmed room, I was on my computer as usual when my father walked in and ...... startled me into closing my computer.

"Hey, Gary. Let's have a talk," he said. I turned my back on him, scratching my head. "No, there is nothing to talk about. Just leave me alone.'

He lightly hugged me from behind and let go. I was so upset and sad at myself for being so pathetic. Elbows on the desk, I covered my eyes and started sobbing."

All of our ears in the entire classroom were completely riveted by his story, waiting for his next words. In this spur of the moment, I knew that this was going to be a great lecture today.

He continued, "and then my father said, 'Even if everyone rejects you, even if you have no one left to stand for you, your mother and I still love you. You know what, Gary? Do you know how I started my own business and built it as large as it is today? We haven't had a chance to talk about it like this until now. When I was graduating from college, I applied to over a hundred different companies but got rejected by all of them. You see, day after day, rejection letters kept being delivered to my mailbox. It made me feel defeated. No one needs me, I thought. Was it because I wasn't as handsome as..... Harrison Ford?

I blamed my mother as if it was her fault for my unattractive appearance. But then, I reconsidered it from a different perspective, 'God is giving me a chance to start my own business. While everyone else is just working for someone else, I have a chance to work for myself, become a president of a company, and be the one to hire others. In order for me to make it come true, I had to learn more and gain something on my own, not just wait for someone to give me something one day. As a result, putting my bitter experience to use, I started a recruiting company. At first, I only had two employees. They were both outcasts from society. But now, we have 2,000 employees. We were able to provide the service that matched the needs of the time. It wasn't only me, but lots of other people were also struggling everywhere, just like me.

Listen to me, Gary. When you confront difficulties, turn them into a positive thought. That's what turns you into a valuable person. Failure is nothing. Life is full of failures. Failures make us aware of our problems. Worthless people are those who don't face any problems, and who don't even bother. You've suffered enough. You're standing at a turning point in your life, about to grasp a great opportunity.'

.......and after a few moments of silence, he added, 'I guess you probably don't need to be told.' and walked out of my room. He didn't mention a single word about the ultra-extremists' website that I was looking at. I think my father has always had faith in me, or also it is possible that he actually did not, but I am certain that it was my parents who suffered more than I did.

If it were not for my father's words, I might have become a "worthy" terrorist. I think many of them are just like us, seeking someone to praise them. There might be various reasons why they wanted to join terrorist groups. I believe that we should look into those reasons and provide methods and education at least to thaw their frozen hearts and unwind their brainwashing....... That's what I think because I don't think my experience was unusual. Anyone could have the same or similar experience. There must be such young people whose failure caused them to drift in the wrong direction. That's why terrorist groups can add new members every day, continuing vandalism. What they are destroying is their own miserable minds occupying their thoughts every day. If they bomb whenever they feel miserable, all decent countries will vanish. It would lead to the end of the world. I am studying again to become one of the people who tackle this problem. That's what I believe."

The room fell silent for a moment. Gary stood there awkwardly. Then, after a few seconds, one of the students stood up and began to applaud loudly. In an instant, the room was filled with thunderous applause. Gary was asked for handshakes or patted on his head messing up his hair. I was extremely happy. I was grateful to his father, and I was also impressed that he had become mature enough to consider the feelings of parents watching over their child who was in danger and at a turning point.

"Sir, Professor François."

Ken, in that yellow sweater, raised his hand up high.

"Yes, Ken. Everyone, please sit down so he can share his opinion."

He started, "I've come to realize something after listening to their opinions. Learning various things and then asking my own heart will, one day, lead me to find what I am looking for. Even I, a peace-loving person, would find something to be concerned about and care enough to change. Now I feel like I can do it. I have confidence that even I can do it. I am glad that I had a chance to attend this lecture.

The students erupted in thunderous applause. Ken scratched his head feeling shy.

I was pleased with this class. Ken, Anita, and Gary. All of them had wonderful things to say.

"You guys are all great students. Ken said earlier about asking his own heart, didn't he? Right. When you have a clear idea of what you want to do, go for it. No matter what anyone says, just stick with it. It may not always go well. You may fail at times or even decide to quit. However, when you overcome such hardships, you will have learned something from them for sure. You can use that as food for thought and take another step forward.

Now, let me tell you about my interesting experience. When I was young, I worked as a cook in a French restaurant. My culinary studies eventually led me to political philosophy, which is why I am now standing in front of you and giving you a lecture. There was one particular event that opened this path for me. Today, I would like to share this story with you.

There was a man named Shusuke Maeda. He was Japanese, like Ken, but lived about 150 years ago. The story is about him saving a tiny village, which resulted in creating one of the greatest food cultures in the world."

Chapter 3

Maeda Itacho

I used to work as a cook. One day, as I was checking to see if the steak was done, my thoughts drifted off to the memory of the Kobe beef that I had tasted when I was young. Unfortunately, due to my musing, the steak was overcooked. Seeing that, our chubby chef's face turned red while my fellow cooks stood still in silence with white faces.

I mumbled to the charred steak.

"When the meat itself has a good flavor, you don't need any sauce to mask it. The sauce should be simply for enhancing the good flavor of the meat, but this sauce makes everything taste the same."

In response to my words, the chef just nodded knowingly without saying anything, as if he understood what I meant. It seemed that his blood pressure was no longer too high. Quickly, he ordered another cook to prepare a fillet steak for him, and he began grilling it in a pan by himself. When it was done, he handed the dish to the server. Our guest seemed quite satisfied with the excellent steak and wine. However, while the chef was watching the guests enjoying their dinner, his face wore a grim expression, standing with his arms crossed in front of his chest. Then, without even turning around, he sensed me standing behind him and told me, "You need to go to Japan immediately, Mr. François, and learn about Kuroge Wagyu (Japanese Black cattle).

A week later, I was at Narita Airport. Pushing my way through the crowds of people from various origins, I headed for the French Embassy, which the chef had referred me to.

I took the Tokyo Metro line to Hiroo station and walked along Gaien Nishi Dori down to the Keio Kindergarten. I had been here several times when I was younger and was fond of the atmosphere of this urban oasis. As I turned left at the kindergarten, and a modern building with all-glass walls appeared. Unknowingly, I stopped walking to admire the building, which turned out to be the French Embassy, my destination. They must have remodeled the building, I assumed, because it looked completely different than I remembered.

I was to work there as an apprentice cook for a while. As if he was expecting me, as soon as the gatekeeper saw me, he walked toward me and admitted me upon checking my passport. Perhaps because of its all-glass exterior, the building looked modern on the outside, but once I stepped inside, the view from the corridor was so integrated with the trees outside that it was as if being in an urban jungle.

The ambassador looked so young as if he was still in his forties. His deep gray suit was made of fine silk, coordinated with a bright red tie. He greeted me with a friendly smile as if we were old friends.

He told me that at the end of March, there would be a social gathering of the ambassadors visiting Ise Jingu Shrine and over Japanese cuisine. When I told him that the head chef had advised me to learn about Japanese Kuroge Wagyu beef, he promised to make a special arrangement for me to join the ambassadors' social gathering.

On that day, the approach to Ise Jingu Shrine was overflowing with crowds of visitors. In front of a teahouse, there was a rice cake fast pounding show, for which people were cheering as the performers shouted in a powerful cadence. As a group of ambassadors was entering the approach with their securities with elaborate precautions, the red "Keep Out" tape moved the crowd to the edge of the street. Even so, the cadence from the fast pounding of rice cakes continued.

People came out, even from inside their stores to welcome us, smiling and waving. I've been wondering why Japanese people smile at all times.

I noticed that the lanterns along the road leading to the shrine had the Japanese sixteen-petal chrysanthemum seal and the Israeli six-pointed star engraved on the top and bottom. When I pointed that out, the Israeli ambassador beside me smiled and told me that some historians believed it was proof that their ancestors had come to Japan on a mission from God. I found it a very interesting story.

After passing through a large torii gate, we came to a gravel road. The sun was shining through the giant cedar trees, whose trunks were so thick that it would take two or three adults to encircle it with their arms... I could hear the gagaku music, a type of Japanese classical music, from the far side of the path. This place reminded me of how it should feel to be refreshed. A lady in white kimono approached and guided us to take a seat on the wooden bench. Each ambassador sat down with their wife.

Matcha tea and Japanese sweets were served at the table. The matcha bowl was called an "Ido Chawan," a special type of tea bowl that gradually soaked up the matcha on the inside but did not leak out its contents. For us chefs, someone who specializes in culinary art, the serving plates and dishes are a subject of study as well. After enjoying the Jingu shrine with the ambassadors, we were escorted to a nearby hotel where the Japanese cuisine dinner party would take place. At the party, I took pictures of each dish and took detailed notes of the unique tastes. The ambassadors were exchanging their critiques about the food without even a second glance at me.

Before too long, the "Matsuzaka beef" had been served. Five pieces of thick, about two-centimeter cubes of steak, were placed on a rusty colored bronze-like plate. From one angle, the plate looked glossy brown, or from another angle, it looked bluish. It was a perfect plate to enhance the beautiful appearance of the red and white marbled meat. Plates are supposed to play a supporting role yet are worth eye entertainment at the same time. I asked the server about the plates they used for serving the steak. He told me that they were called "Seiran Yamato ware," which I had never heard of, but I would like to visit their studio someday.

Four kinds of sauce were brought to the table. The yuzu ponzu (citrus soy vinegar) from Tokushima Koyadaira has the richest aroma and is the best in the world. Wasabi, the rock salt mixed with sansho (Japanese pepper), and the hotel's secret house sauce. I tasted each of them. The secret sauce was made of mirin, a light soy sauce, dashi (soup stock), sake, and something else... I was not sure what it was, but I could taste a subtle tartness within the sweetness.

Green citrus peels were floating in it, so it might be lime, or maybe sudachi citrus. While I was studying the sauces, a sweet aroma wafted out from the steak. With the surface just cooked enough, I put it straight into my mouth. The strong sweet flavor of the meat spread in my mouth. Then, I tried it with each sauce. I see! These sauces were only to enhance and bring out the flavor of the meat. It was different from French cuisine, where we let the meat soak up the sauce to enjoy the flavor of the sauce. However, the meat melted in my mouth before I could chew it. Since I was used to eating chewy meat, it did not satisfy me very much but rather made me crave more steak.

As I enjoyed the taste of the steak with each sauce enhancing its flavor with my left brain as well, I completely forget that I was still at the dinner party.

Looking around and remembering where I was, suddenly laughter and conversations of the ambassadors came back to my consciousness. I was concentrating on the taste with a grim face when the sommelier approached and poured me a fruity fragranced Daiginjo (rice wine) into a slender wine glass. While serving me, he said, "Good food has the power to bring people together." I saw ambassadors of countries that weren't in close relationships, smiling and talking to each other over dinner. The U.S. ambassador in a white suit with a red tie, as if to resemble the Japanese flag, said in a loud, husky voice, "You know, when I was young, I was stationed in Kobe. I can never forget the taste of Kobe beef cutlet sandwiches I had there. The juicy meat and the crispy batter spread in my mouth, and the grill-marked buns wrapped its flavor just right." Putting his hands together on his chin, he shared his delicious experience using such a mouth-watering expression, that everyone smiled at him.

Then, the hotel manager said, "Later, let us serve each of our guests a bite-size Kobe beef sandwich."

At his courtesy, the ambassadors all smiled happily, and a flicker of excitement arose among the guests. Shortly after, the sandwiches were brought first to the American Ambassador.

"Was it like this?" the server asked anxiously. The Ambassador took a bite, and with the second bite, the sandwich had already disappeared.

"This is it! This is how I remembered. Everyone, please try it." The server was relieved and went back to the kitchen to bring the rest out for everyone. The pleasant aroma of toasted bread combined with the sweet scent of oil and deep-fried crispy batter, and the thick-cut steak, all of those made one special sandwich. Although the meat was tender enough to bite through with ease, it didn't lose its body, and then the sweet aroma of juices overwhelmed my taste buds. Fine ketchup added a little tartness to it for perfection. I could totally understand why the American ambassador had so highly praised this sandwich.

I took a few photos of each dish as it was served. Before dessert was served, I asked the server if I could meet the Japanese chef. He said, "Since he'd finished preparing for dessert, he can spare twenty minutes or so before his greeting to our guests." I apologized to the French ambassador sitting next to me for excusing myself to follow the server to the kitchen.

Now that all the hustle, bustle, and busiest time was over, the kitchen staff seemed more relaxed and welcomed me with a warm greeting. The server introduced me to the head chef, or as they call him in Japanese cuisine, "Itacho," Mr. Maeda. Mr. Maeda was about 160 centimeters tall, small build, and wearing a warm smile on his face. I got straight to the point, asking him about the secret of the taste of Wagyu beef. I had studied in Japan before, so I could understand some Japanese and still speak a little.

Maeda Itacho brought out two blocks of meat. One was Aussie beef, and the other was Kuroge Wagyu. Anyone even without any culinary knowledge could easily tell which was which. He handed me a pair of thin, transparent plastic gloves to wear and began to explain about Wagyu beef.

The white fat streaks in the lean meat are called "Sashi ("marbling" in English), he said. He told me to lightly press down on both blocks of meat with my index finger. I pressed down on the Aussie beef. Holding it for a while, I wasn't sure what kind of experiment it was, so I looked at the itacho's face. The itacho smiled and told me to press the Wagyu beef with the same amount of pressure. Within a minute, the white fat around the meat began to melt away. I looked into the itacho's eyes in surprise.

He said, "This sashi starts to melt at about 17 degrees Celsius. That is why it melts when you put it in your mouth. Melted sashi on the tongue blends the flavor of the meat and the subtle sweet aroma of the fat together to create 'umami,' which spreads in your mouth. It contains a lot of monounsaturated fatty acids that are good for the human body. It is genetic. There are various names of Japanese branded beef based on the region of production, such as Matsuzaka beef from Mie, Kobe beef, that I made a sandwich with earlier, from Kobe, Miyazaki, Awaji, Yonezawa, Omi, and so on."

Eagerly taking notes, I further asked him why each region could grow its own excellent brand name beef. He ordered his subordinate cook to put the meat in a specialized refrigerator, pointing just one finger to do so, and then continued.

"Well, they actually all come from one type of cattle. The calves are born in the mountains of Ojiro or Muraoka, located 700 to 800 meters above sea level in the town of Kami-cho, Mikata-gun, in the Tajima region of northern Hyogo Prefecture. They drink mineral-rich fine water which springs from the rocks. After a year of careful rearing, the calves are shipped out to various places. Then, they are properly reared for a few more years, before being given their own brand name.

"So, you are saying that all the cattle were originally born and raised in Tajima region?"

"Yes, that is correct, Mr. François. Ninety-nine point nine percent of the Wagyu beef on the market are purebred Tajima cattle."

It was a fascinating fact. It made me want to see Tajima cattle with my own eyes and learn more about where and how they are raised. But I had never seen Kuroge wagyu, to begin with, nor been to the Tajima region before, so I was not familiar with the area.

"In fact, my ancestor, Shusuke Maeda, was the first person to establish the foundation of the Tajima cattle, so-called 'vine,' or lineage. However, back then, Japanese people did not customarily eat beef. Cows were only valued as a workforce for agriculture, or service cattle. It was only about a hundred years ago that people realized that they were the best beef cattle in Japan."

He explained carefully.

"Oh, yeah, the story of Shusuke Maeda became a movie. If you are interested. I can show you the DVD later."

I gratefully accepted his offer without a moment of hesitation. I could hardly contain my excitement. After the dinner party, Maeda itacho invited me to watch the DVD in a hotel room with a big-screen TV. The title was *Run! Shusuke.* I never thought that this single film would change my life for good......

Chapter 4

Run! Shusuke

A boy at the age of seven or eight kept talking to a cow endlessly. To my surprise, all of those cows were black cattle. One inky black cow was staring at the boy with its round eyes.

It was a very quiet cow, not even making any "moo" sounds like the other cows. The boy rolled up his fine printed kimono by tucking its hem into his belt, showing his bare legs. He was holding a bundle of straw in his hand and scrubbing the cow's neck.

"Hana, yesterday, I went to the temple school for the first time. I learned 'Iroha-ni-hoheto.' I pretended I was a monk and chanted like this, 'I-Ro-Ha-Ni Ho-He-To…,' with a ringing sound of the singing bowl. It's easier to remember that way. Then, everyone said I was a genius, and we all chanted together with the bell. Hey, do you like it? It's good to be nice and clean, isn't it?"

The boy gazed with pleasure at the way the cows' black coats glowed a deep purple like velvet and then gave them hay piled up in the corner of the shed in pieces so that they could eat it at ease.

"Eat as much as you can. It's good. I need to go to school now, so please wait for me."

"Shusuke!"

Suddenly, a woman's voice came rattling from the main house, yelling loudly. She seemed to be the boy's mother.

"I knew you would be here again. I told you that you didn`t need to come to the stable today. Finish your breakfast now. I can't clean up if you don't," she said.

His mother was young and seemed to be still in her twenties with a slender face and distinguishing features. Also, her teeth were naturally straight.

Shusuke argued back, "I have to feed them first before eating my breakfast. But mom, why don't I have to come to the stable today? They wait for me every day."

She replied, "I said there is no need today, no need. Rather, you need to eat your breakfast and go to the temple school."

She brushed the straw dust off Shusuke's kimono.

He said, "I still have plenty of time before going to school, so I don't have to be in such a hurry."

His mother rolled her eyes and said, "Well then, go to school early today and help them clean the temple, too," crossing her arms with frustration.

Shusuke looked flummoxed for a moment but argued back to her insistently.

"But we'll all do that when we're done each day. You are acting strange today, mom."

With that, his mother finally lost her patience, grabbed Shusuke by the collar of his kimono, and started to walk away.

"Enough is enough. You need to eat your breakfast now."

Before stepping into the house, she exchanged a glance with a man who appeared to be her husband hiding in the storage shed. Making sure Shusuke entered his house, the man stepped quickly inside the stable on tiptoe, taking his place. He put the reins through the metal ring that ran through the nose of the eight-month-old calf that Shusuke had just been taking care of just a few moments ago, pushed it out of the shed, and walked down the narrow path in front of the house. Without making a sound, the calf walked at the same pace as the man. Unlike horses, cows do not like to be pulled by force and will resist and pull back if you try. To get them to walk on their own, you have to follow them from the side or walk slightly behind. He was relieved that he had successfully escaped from Shusuke's eyes, but the mother cow left behind in the shed must have sensed something. It suddenly slammed against the shed making a rattling noise and cried out a high-pitched "Moo!" Her mother's cry made the calf try to turn around, but then the man tugged hard on the reins and struck it squarely on its rump with a thin bamboo stick. Reluctantly, the calf trudged forward again, but as if she was searching for her mother, her ears were twitching restlessly from side to side.

Wondering what the calf's round black eyes were seeing and how it felt, the man stopped walking and stroked its forehead while looking into its eyes. He felt pity for the little calf as it turned away and looked down at the ground, but to shake off this feeling, he tightened the reins even more and started walking again.

Meanwhile, Shusuke was rushing his meal, shoveling rice into his mouth. He immediately noticed a commotion in the stable.

"Mom, I hear a noise coming from the cow stable. What's going on? I'll go check on them." Then, he hurried out of the house without finishing his breakfast, leaving his chopsticks scattered on the tatami floor.

"No, Shusuke!"

Startled, his mother quickly stood up to try to grab his arm but failed, so she ran after him.

"Shusuke, you can't go that way. Come back now," she yelled.

Shusuke put on his straw sandals in a hurry and rushed out to the cowshed.

The cow looked bewildered and upset, but when Shusuke rubbed its neck saying, "there, there," in a conciliatory tone, it gradually settled down and became quiet.

"Are you crying?" asked Shusuke.

Shusuke read the expression on the Cow's face and turned around with a start. Hana, the calf he had been petting earlier, was gone. His face turned pale. Instantly, he rushed out of the stable and run down the path in front of the house, shouting "Hanaaaaa!" His mother caught up with him and held him in a wrestling full nelson hold.

"Please wait, Shusuke," she said appealingly.

He resisted. "She is my Hana. Where are you taking my Hana?" He cried with a trembling voice.

"No, Shusuke. Shusuke, I can't let you go!"

While his mother tried to hold him with all of her strength, he continued to struggle and soon escaped from her grip, and finally started running as fast as he could.

"Hana, Hana! Don't take Hana away from me! She's my cow!"

His shrill voice reached the man's ears in distance. Shusuke's father, Izaemon, clicked his tongue and muttered, "That brat." Hana was about to walk in the direction of Shusuke's voice, but Izaemon didn't let her, wrapping the reins around his right elbow. Shusuke kicked his sandals off as he chased after her. In response to Shusuke's voice, Hana began to moo a few times. Shusuke ran shouting "Hanaaaaaa," but he tripped and fell to the ground. Immediately, he tried to get up; however, the shadows of his father and the calif were getting further and further away.

"Hanaaaaa! Nooooo! Dad, you are a jerk!"

Shusuke plopped down on the ground and cried, wiping his runny nose with his sleeve.

A moment later, the ground began to shake and thud. Shusuke looked up and saw Hana running toward him dragging the reins behind her. He was so astonished to see Hana running at full speed that he could not stand up. Izaemon was hurriedly chasing after her.

"Watch out! Shusuke, get out of the way!"

Bawling at the top of his lungs, Izaemon ran toward Shusuke stumbling over his own feet, but when Hana came near Shusuke, she suddenly stopped running and slowly walked up to him. Then, she put her nose close to Shusuke's cheek. He wiped his tear-stained face with his kimono sleeve and put his hand around Hana's neck. Overwhelmingly happy, he called her name, "Hana, Hana" over and over.

A big man, Izaemon arrived breathlessly and gave a hard slap to Shusuke. His small body flew into the air and hit the ground. Witnessing this instantaneous event, Hana was so agitated that she was kicking the ground with one foot while moving her head up and down.

"You moron! I told you not to name any cows!"

Shusuke's mother finally caught up with them. Izaemon was about to strike Shusuke again with his clenched fist, but she intervened and covered her son to protect him.

"Hun, he is still a little boy, so please stop now. That was enough. I promise that I'll talk with him. "

Shusuke burst out crying, and Hana was staring at him. Then suddenly, she turned to the side, walked a few steps, and came back to Shusuke with a piece of green foxtail in her mouth. He took it and patted her neck gently. She knelt on her front feet, gesturing for him to hop on. When he clung to Hana's neck trying to ride on her back, Izaemon helped him sit on her neck. Shusuke wagged the green foxtail from side to side and hummed a nursery rhyme about crows. Pleased, his mother was looking back as she pulled Hana by the reins, singing along with him. Cawing crows were flying in the sky in the opposite direction of the setting sun.

"Well, I guess you win. You little cowherd"

Izaemon said with a wry smile.

Chapter 5

Tajima's Mountain Cattle

"Come on, Oyoshi, hurry up. It's happening any minute now. We'll have a new calf."

The little "Cowherd Boy" had grown into a tall young man with a well-formed nose. Shusuke married Oyoshi, who was the daughter of the wealthiest man in the village. She was well known for her beauty, with fair skin and an oval face.

She pulled up the hem of her kimono and sat beside Shusuke, holding her breath.

A moment later, the mother cow let out a high-pitched cry, and then there was a thud as something fell onto the straw. Shifting their bodies to the side, they saw a small black object covered with an amniotic membrane wriggling around. The mother cow stretched out her neck and bit through the translucent membrane. Then, as if it couldn't wait any longer, the calf, whose entire body was wet and gleaming black, emerged from inside wiggling all four limbs. It was eager to stand up but kept falling a few times. After the fourth trial, it managed to stand up at last, even though it was still struggling to keep standing on its trembling legs. Yet, after a while, the trembling stopped, and it began to suckle its mother's belly even without being instructed to do so.

"It's all good now."

Shusuke was even happier to know that the calf was a female.

(Today, bulls are valued more because they have more meat, but back then, bulls were only valued as service cattle. Therefore, since females were more obedient and patient than males, they were traded for a much higher price.)

"Good job, Koume. You did a great job."

Shusuke had named this mother cow "Koume."

"I've been taking care of her like she's my own child since she was little, so I know what she's trying to say," he said.

Oyoshi immediately answered back, "Oh, dear honey, you take care of them more than your own children, don't you? Even on the day of the most important family celebration, you were in the cowshed, and the money we had saved up for that occasion has turned into a cow."

Shusuke was a little upset and denied her words.

"That's not true at all. Of course, I love my kids without any doubt. Don't worry. Our kids have you, Oyoshi, so I'm counting on you."

Shusuke bowed his head a little and wiped his face with the towel wrapping around his neck, feeling embarrassed.

Oyoshi rolled her eyes, expressing "Oh well, that's a good enough excuse."

"Fine, that's all right. I married a man who had been known by the nickname of 'Cowherd Boy,' so I've already accepted what's to come."

A few days passed. The calf grew up to have a fine coat, nice sturdy heel angles, and good muscles to stand on. As Shusuke was examining the calf from various angles, it approached him tentatively and started licking his hand. He stroked its nose and said, "You are such a good calf, just like your mom. You are great. You see, the hind legs need to be sturdy to pull the farm equipment. You're ......, 'Sato,' that's your name. My father was really upset and scolded me badly when I named cows, but to me, it feels natural to call you by your name.

The villagers were working with black cattle on the small, terraced rice farms. A stout middle-aged man was watching them in a distance, fanning his face with his hat, trying to beat the heat. He came to visit Shusuke. He was a well-known Dai-bakuro (cattle and horse broker) from Osaka. Just then, he saw the seven- or eight-month-old "Sato" that Shusuke was walking with and decided to talk to him.

"Well, well.... Tajima's cows are really impressive as I'd expected. This one also has good muscles. Hey, Shusuke, would you sell me this calf in two months? I'll pay whatever price you wish."

"Whatever I wish? No exception?"

"Yeah, I'm sure your cows are really good and won't go wrong, so I'll take them regardless of the price, no matter how expensive that is. Even so, I can sell it for an even higher price, no doubt. I'm positive."

As stroking Sato's forehead, Shusuke hushed her, she calmed down and stood still.

"I see," he said, "I've been raising her as my family, but this calf can be sold for what I think she's worth."

The offer sounds too good to be true. He looked into the broker's eyes.

"Well, what do you say?" The man asked.

Shusuke answered, "Heck no. I won't sell her. But when she grows up a little older, I'll check out the Bakuro market in Osaka to see how other cattle are and compare how good this one is. "

Hearing Shusuke's words, the broker was pleased that it would be a great chance to introduce Ojiro's cows to the public.

He replied, "Sounds good. You will learn how great Tajima cows are. It will amaze everyone at the market for sure. I'll come with you."

"All right, then. Let's test out my herding skill," said Shusuke.

It seems that the man was also smitten with her. He stroked the hair on her neck. Sato was obedient, letting him do as he pleased.

A few months later, Shusuke took Sato, who was no longer a calf but a young heifer now, to the market in Osaka with the Dai-bakuro as his guide. Many fine cows were at the market. It was the first time for Shusuke to see such a big market. He tied Sato to a log stake and looked around at all the other cows. He found cows that were too tired to stand up, that had poor muscles in their front legs, that were violent-tempered, and that kept mooing constantly…. There were various types of cattle.

As he was observing the other cows, they called out a number, and a cow assigned with that number was pulled around in a circle. Brokers and farmers surrounded the cow, and the bidding started. They auctioned cows one after another.

Soon, it was Sato's turn. Shusuke stepped into the center of the circle and called out, "Oo-yo!" to Sato. She stopped her motion and stood still. Although she was small in stature, she had a shiny fur coat, stood with a very good posture, and showed no signs of fatigue. Her regal posture caught everyone's eye.

When Shusuke said to her, "Hachi-hachi," she began to walk to the left. Then, he said, "Choi-choi," and slowly, she began to walk along the edge of the ring. Everyone gasped at how obedient and smart she was. Of course, he had no intention to sell Sato, but he set the starting price very high, taking into account the broker's advice.

"Okay, we will start with eight hundred monme. One *ryo, one ryo and three hundred, one ryo and five hundred, one ryo and eight hundred, and yes, two ryo....Anyone else?" The auctioneer of the market called out the bids in a lively voice pointing to each bidder with his finger.

"Two ryo and five hundred, two ryo and five hundred, three ryo.... Anyone else? Then the winning bid will be for three ..."

"Hold on, three ryo and five hundred!"

To everyone's surprise, it was Shusuke who shouted at last. The auctioneer immediately replied, "You mean, you're going to buy it back? Anybody else? Okay then, sold for three ryo and five hundred!"

Shusuke won the bid.

"Wow, that is the Shusuke's cow from Ojiro. It's very impressive. I'm glad that I had a chance to see it today."

"Oh well. Too bad. I didn't expect that the seller himself would buy it back."

* "Ryo" was an old large Japanese currency.

"Shusuke's cows never seem to stop increasing in value. Next time, I'll be the winning bidder"

"Are you kidding? It's me who is going to win."

People at the market kept talking about his cattle, which certainly entertained Shusuke.

"Well, well, well, there's no need to quarrel. Why don't we visit Ojiro together?"

"Sure, let's do that. How soon we can go?"

Although Ojiro was a tiny village, Ojiro's cattle prices went up almost four times higher than the asking price. As a result, however, Shusuke ended up owing the market a huge amount of money in order to buy Sato back. It was the first time Shusuke's cattle were recognized by the brokers as "Tajima's Yamadashi cattle" (Mountain Cattle from the Tajima region).

Shusuke and his father Izaemon were watching the village from the cattle shed adjacent to the main house entrance. Shusuke reported to his father what had happened at the market. He wanted to brag about his cattle being valued much higher than he had asked for, but it meant that he also had to tell him about the money he owed to the market. With some mixed feelings, he began blabbering away while his body stiffened.

"Dad, people valued her at the highest, the best among all, and she won first prize, but I had no choice but to borrow money from the market to buy her back."

Izaemon was listening calmly until he heard the last part of Shusuke's confession, and soon his face turned red with anger.

"Are you serious? You big idiot! You just fell for the broker's line."

Shusuke was bracing himself for an iron fist to fly at him, but to his surprise, his father looked down and muttered reluctantly, "Oh well. We just have to cut down a few 50-year-old cedars in the forest."

Chapter 6

Ume's Death

Just then, Matabei, a neighbor, came running to the cowshed and, upon spotting Shusuke, shouted out loudly under his breath, "Shusuke, please! Please help us!" He cried, "My daughter has a really high fever and is deathly ill. We don't have enough money to take her to a doctor. Please, oh please, lend me some money, I beg you."

"Your little Ume! Okay, I got it. I will bring a doctor to your house right away."

"Thank you, thank you so much. We have snow now in the valley, so I'll go out to the town to earn some money to pay you back, I promise."

 During the evening, snow began to flutter in the valley of Ojiro. Shusuke pulled the old doctor by the hand and hurried to Matabei's house. There, he spotted an impressive cow tethered to their gappy ramshackle house. In the straw-paved living room, Matabei's wife, Kayo, was applying a cold piece of cloth to the forehead of their five-year-old daughter, Ume. She was covered with a flimsy blanket, muttering, "Mom, Dad," through chattering teeth with vacant eyes. Kayo wrapped her hands around her daughter's little hands on the verge of tears, calling out, "Ume, we are here, mommy and daddy are here," and cuddled her gently.

The doctor hurried to sit beside Ume, put his ears on her chest to listen to her heart, and took her pulse. Then, he muttered in a low voice avoiding eye contact with her parents, "Why didn't you do anything when she first became ill?"

The color drained from Kayo's face. She asked the doctor in a quavering voice.

"Doctor, my daughter is…"

He shook his head. "Her cold got worse, and now……she won't……Mom, hug her close to your heart."

Kayo began to sob. Mumbling, "Ume, Ume," she put her daughter on her lap, opened her ragged kimono over her chest to wrap around Ume, and held her tightly in her arms. Kayo pressed her cheek against Ume's limp face, and her tears flowed unceasingly, soaking Ume's face.

"Ume, it's my fault. It's all my fault. We had no choice but to send you out to serve when the spring would come, instead of our cow. If this is punishment for thinking to give you up at such a young age, why you, Ume? Couldn't I take your place?"

"Mom, I….I love your smile…so, please don't cry……"

Soon after Ume spoke in a weak feeble voice, her arm lost its strength and dropped heavily onto Kayo's lap. Seeing this, Kayo and Matabei called out Ume's name over and over, but she did not even twitch. Kayo and Matabei sat beside their daughter and wept uncontrollably.

Other villagers saw Shusuke running with the doctor and followed them to Matabei's doorstep and watched them while praying.

Shusuke stood there clenching his fists in regret. Tarobei, a fifteen-year-old neighbor, let out a holler-like cry and slammed the hoe he was carrying to the ground. The villagers turned to Tarobei.

"My father, too, fell off a ladder to his death when he went away to work outside of this village. My family won't survive if I don't work. I hate this poor village. I can't live like this anymore. I'm going to get out of here," he said, fell to the ground rubbing his head against it, and cried out loudly. Everyone hung their heads. The fear for their lives that they all felt became evident because of Ume's death and Tarobei's words.

It was getting dark outside. With a lantern in his hand, the doctor left Matabei's house. As he was passing Shusuke, he turned to him and said, "Everyone around this area is the same. They can't afford to see a doctor even though I always tell them I won't charge them……Those tiny, terraced fields can barely produce enough to feed themselves. Illness can be cured if they treat it early on......Yet, they had to send a little girl like her away to work......It's a shame."

Shusuke walked away without a word and strode with a broad step to the top of the hill where there was a single cherry tree. Oyoshi trotted after him. Standing on the hill, Shusuke looked out over the village, where no smoke from the cooking stoves was seen, even in the evening. For a member of the Maeda family, the mountain owner family, the life of the villagers was beyond his imagining. -- *Why had I never looked at the village without smoke in the evening before, and what was I looking at ...... cows?* True. He was stunned to realize that all he had seen were cows. Shusuke clenched his teeth and held back his tears.

"Oyoshi. I've decided to become a Dai-bakuro, a successful cow broker. I'm going to make this village a major cattle-producing area. We will make good draft cattle and sell them. I'm going to make this village the biggest cattle ranch in Japan, and then the residents of this village will be able to live without suffering." He said this in a serious tone of voice. Oyoshi knew that it was a big decision for him, so she asked him to confirm it.

"Can you make such a fantastic dream come true?"

Shusuke answered firmly, looking straight ahead at the village of Ojiro.

"Someone must do something to help eliminate this poverty. I learned from the market in Osaka. By observing only once, I can tell how outstanding these Tajima cows are compared with others. Now, what we must do is to consistently produce good cattle to sell calves at a high price every year. Oyoshi, I believe the meaning of our lives, as humans, is to live for others."

Looking at him from the side, Oyoshi fell in love with him once again. At the same time, she felt her body filled with strength.

"You are the best cowherd boy in Japan. You have to do something to prevent a tragedy like that of Ume from happening anymore."

"Yes..."

Shusuke placed a few white chrysanthemum flowers on a tiny grave in front of

Matabei's house and joined his hands together in prayer. The grave was merely heaped with earth. Then, he turned around to speak to Matabei.

"Matabei, I'm truly sorry for your loss. It was a devastating incident. How is Kayo holding up?"

"Thank you, Shusuke. We have to work to eat. Kayo has gone out to the farm. I have to take our cow with me now, too. Could I ask you to give us a little time to pay you back for the doctor's bill? We have snow now, so this would be the last time to work on the farm before spring. Then, I'll go out to work down in the city."

Matabei pulled off the cloth towel from his head and bowed sincerely.

"Nah, no worries. The doctor didn't even give her any medicine. He said it was fine."

Years passed by. Shusuke saw Matabei and his wife working on their farm several times, but for some reason, he was hesitant to visit them. However, today was the third anniversary of Ume's death. Shusuke decided to visit their house bringing chrysanthemums to put on Ume's grave.

"Hey, Matabei. These are for Ume. Also, may I take a look at your cow?"

Ever since he saw their good-looking cow when he stopped by for Ume's memorial service, he had been always curious about that young cow. When they entered the cowshed located next to the house entrance, the small cow looked at Shusuke silently.

"Here she is. She is filling the empty place of our daughter. She works very hard without any complaints."

Matabei was very proud of his cow. Shusuke walked around the cow to check her thoroughly, patted her on the shoulder, and commented, "Matabei, this is quite a fine-looking cow. The muscles in her front legs are taut, her shoulders are well-developed, and she has a gentle disposition. ....Matabei, would you sell her to me for your asking price?"

"Oh, sorry but no, I can't do that even if it's your wish. We can't do farm work without her. Besides, it is a memento of Ume."

"I see. ......Then, how about if I buy this cow from you and lend it to you, Matabei?"

"Well, that.... that would be a great help. I've been having trouble coming up with the money to pay for the cow since Ume passed away, and we couldn't send her to work anymore. That would be a great help. Are you sure about this, Shusuke?"

"Yes, of course, sure thing. Instead, when this cow births a calf, take care of it, would you? Then, when the time comes, I will buy the calf at a high price again, so you can sell it to me every year."

"Shusuke, you are letting us borrow your cow, which means the calf of your cow is yours. But are you going to pay for it? Aren't you overpaying us? Isn't it too much for us to accept your kind offer? But if we may, I won't have to go out to work anymore to make a living."

Matabei's face turned into a big smile.

"Sure, let me do that, Matabei. I should have done that when Ume was still alive. I just didn't think of it. I'm sorry. I will take my commission for each calf sold, so don't worry about anything. You know what, I'm going to keep a record of all the cows in the village. Do you know the parents of this heifer?"

"Yes, I do, indeed. Do you see that cow over there? There, Sasuke has three cattle. Mine is the offspring of the one with the best coat and that one there."

"Then, Ume was to work for Sasuke's family?"

"No, she wasn't. Sasuke's calf had already been sold to a big farmer from Awaji Island. But, I really liked the calf and couldn't give her up. So, when the person came from Awaji to pick it up, I dared to ask him if I could keep her. Well, eventually, he let me take her, but in return, he wanted to adopt Ume since they needed extra hands for their work. Probably, he said to 'adopt' her to make it sound more decent, but in reality, to have her serve them in payment for debts."

While talking with Matabei, Shusuke wrote down the cow's age and characteristics and measured its size. After that, he headed over to Sasuke's house with Matabei. Silver grasses and green foxtails were still growing along the roadside. Remembering his childhood, he pulled one of the green foxtails and walked for a while, swinging it from side to side.

Sasuke was just preparing straws for the cows. He was older than Shusuke, but they had known each other since their childhood days at the temple school. Shusuke greeted Sasuke and asked him if he could see his cattle.

"I see. This is the mother of Matabei's cow. Hmmm…She's very good. Her rump seems strong enough to give birth to a lot more calves. Her black coat is nice and shiny, and her skin is soft. She is such a nice cow. And this is the father? …… I see, he's got a nice, tight body."

For a while, Shusuke was checking the cattle by grabbing the skin on their backs and petting them gently. Expectedly, the bull was more aggressive than the female cow, sniffing Shusuke threateningly and pulling its head back to resist when Shusuke approached, but when he gently petted it with an exquisite voice, it suddenly calmed down. It seemed that Sasuke was very happy to hear Shusuke's praise.

He said, "If Shusuke agrees that it's a great cow, then there is no doubt," proudly, rubbing his cow. Then, he pointed to the other cow and asked, "Shusuke, I'm not sure if this one is pregnant or not. Could you take a look at her?"

Shusuke called out to the cow, "Doh-doh" and lifted its tail.

"No need to worry. She's pregnant. She will give birth in the spring, so I will come back to check on her."

"Glad to hear that. Well, I'm counting on you."

"Sure. Hey, Sasuke. Would you consider selling this non-pregnant cow to me? I'll pay whatever the price you'd ask for."

It became his habit whenever he found a good cow.

"What are you saying? Are you serious? Well, if you insist, I'd be grateful if you take her for the price I ask. Another calf is coming soon anyway. How about one ryo?"

As if evaluating Sasuke's three cattle, Shusuke said, "Nah, I'll pay more. Three ryo. If the new calf is also a good one, then I'll buy it, too, so sell it to me. I'll pay as much as I can."

"That would be a great offer. We can live on one calf for a year. By the way, Shusuke, what have you been doing all this time?"

Shusuke answered, "I'm registering all the cattle in the village. By doing this, I can see what kind of cattle are being raised in the village."

"What are you going to do after buying all the good cows in the entire village?"

"I'm studying how to produce the best quality cows and not just once, but constantly every year from Tajima. If we can produce good cattle more often, then we can sell them every year at a high price. I think it would help this village."

"Shusuke, it wouldn't really help our village, would it? Without even working on your farm, you roam around from one cow to another. Some people even scornfully laugh at you. 'That cowherd boy has lost his mind,' they say. Don't you feel bad for Oyoshi?"

--I knew it would come to this.

Shusuke thought. Even though I do things for others with good intentions, some people bad-mouth me. When a bakuro (broker) doesn't have much experience or good achievements, people criticize him, but once he becomes successful with lots of great results, they become jealous of him. He learned it the hard way. But to shake off his annoyance, he was accustomed to saying, "Sure, sure." After all, I must not be concerned about what others say in order to follow my heart. No matter what, I must do what I believe is right. If I feel sorry for those who are jealous or talk behind my back, I will not be upset. Little by little, Shusuke's temper had softened.

"Oh, sure, sure. Let them laugh at me. As long as they cooperate with me like this, that's all that matters to me."

At first, he had started to say, "Sure, sure," to suppress his anger, but now his words were truly meant, "It's only a tiny matter. I appreciate your help even just a little," expressing his humble gratitude. From then on, Shusuke left the care of the cows to his family as much as possible. Meanwhile, even during the extreme summer heat, he visited every single house in the village with a towel hanging around his neck to take inventory of how their cows were growing. When they were ready, he took them to the market as a bakuro.

Chapter 7

Shusuke's Ambivalence

Shusuke had already turned forty-five years old. Upon returning home with a heifer, he got down on his knees and begged his father, Izaemon.

"Dad, could you please sell some additional land in the mountains to make more money? I found a good cow, and I bought it."

"You idiot!" Izaemon yelled at Shusuke, throwing the cup of tea that he was drinking at Shusuke's head.

"How many cows does it take to satisfy you? When are you going to stop? Now, we need to build another cowshed since it will be too packed. Oyoshi feeds cows mixed grasses following your formula every day, but…. If you keep buying cows and selling our land each time you buy a new cow, sooner or later, there will be no land to sell."

Shusuke persisted. "All I want to do is to turn this village into a cattle producer so that I can save everyone."

"Don't be such a dreamer."

"Why do you call it a mere dream? It's not just a dream, dad. Do you know how well Tajima cows are regarded? I know what I'm talking about."

"How can you have such confidence?"

"You know, people called me a cowherd boy since I was very little, so I trust my hunch. But dad, it's not enough to have just one good cow that happened to be born and sold at a high price. We have to build trust that 'Tajima cows are always fine and never go wrong.' No matter what, we can only sell the highest quality cows. So, we need to improve the breed so that little to no calves are born below our expected quality. In order for that, I have to know the genealogy of every single cow in the village."

Their relative, Hanjiro Okada peeked out from the back of the house, laughing. "Okay, okay. If Izaemon doesn't want to help you pay for your cow, I'll cut down some of my trees."

Izaemon embarrassedly said, "No, I can't let you do that, Hanjiro," waving his hand.

"Nah, it's all right. The other day, I let Shusuke handle my calf, and he sold it for an unexpectedly high price. It was a huge profit for me, so what he's saying is true. Look at the people in the village. They are all becoming happier than before."

Izaemon was still skeptical. "Sorry to trouble you, too."

"No, no worries. It's nothing at all. I like how Shusuke genuinely thinks about this village. He has been the village's smartest kid ever since he was a child. It's not him if he doesn't do something unexpected."

With a sour face, Izaemon reminded Shusuke slowly in a low voice, "Don't trouble any of your relatives anymore," and disappeared into the back of the house. Hanjirou patted Shusuke on his shoulder, who was still on his knees on the entrance floor, and gently comforted him, "Shusuke, don't mind what your father just said. Even though he said that, at the last meeting, he announced that he would appoint you as the heir to the family after all. You know, despite what he said earlier, your father is the one who supports you the most."

Shusuke bowed deeply to the back of Hanjiro as he left the house.

Seeing Shusuke's hard work, even some villagers who had gathered and mocked him behind his back, gradually began to offer their help, whenever they had spare time. Since he had been working alone without any complaints, this change in atmosphere made him believe that there was nothing impossible with their support. People in the village began to think that perhaps his tremendous dream might turn out to be legitimate and began to follow the same dream as Shusuke.

A "Vortex of Hope" began to swirl. Shusuke paid the highest possible price for calves so that the villagers could enjoy a better life. He put those calves on the market, and Sasuke and Hanjiro came along. Every time, Tajima's calves sold like hot cakes and at the highest price.

"Sasuke, Hanjiro, thanks to you both, they were sold at quite high prices, so let me pay you some commission."

Shusuke pulled out one ryo each from the leather bag that contained twenty-five ryo.

"What are you talking about, Shusuke? You paid a lot more than I'd expected to receive for my calves, so I cannot accept any commissions on top of that. We are only pulling our own calves together. Besides, your portion will be less if you pay us. That's not a good way to run a business."

"Don't mind me. As long as I get paid for the round trip, that's all I ask for," said Shusuke and waved his hand. Hanjiro dismissed, "I don't need any commission. I simply enjoy just being a part of it. Shusuke, you should save up, so you don't make your father upset again."

Shusuke thought of his father for a second.

"You're right. Probably I should do so. Thank you, Hanjiro."

On the way home, Shusuke stopped by Matabei's house.

"Matabei, are you at home?"

"I'm here, in the cowshed. Come on over. Shusuke, it looks like our cow is pregnant again."

Shusuke walked into the cowshed and checked the cow.

"Yap, it's growing well. Matabei, would you sell it to me again? Also, I was able to sell your cow for a higher price, so though it's not much, here is   your additional profit from the sales."

"No, no, Shusuke. That is too much. You have given us enough already."

"Well, buy some flowers for Ume and a comb for Kayo with this money, will you?"

"All right then. I'll take it. Thank you, Shusuke. I'll raise another fine calf, so please come back later and buy it again."

"Yes, I'll be looking forward to it."

Shusuke was more than happy to see that what he had been working on clearly brought back smiles and laughter to villagers and the smoke rising from the chimneys at dinner time.

At the same time though, there was a difficult issue that he was continually facing. Sometimes he went to check the new calves only to discover that they had bad hind legs or bad tempers, in other words, the quality was varying. In such cases, he had to turn down the villagers. To protect the Tajima cow's good reputation, for which buyers trusted that Tajima cows were always of perfect quality, Shusuke could not sell such unqualified calves in the market. Ideally, a family could manage to support themselves for a year by selling just one calf, but with a non-sellable calf, they would struggle for a year to survive.

Reluctantly, he bought those at half price and used them for work in the mountains, yet he knew he could not do that every time. He was struggling to somehow establish a quality strain to avoid going downhill together with the cows, and it needed to be done as soon as possible. However, things didn't go as he'd wished for, and the seasons flew by.

Chapter 8

The Miraculous Cow

As water filled the terraced rice fields, the loud croaking of toads started to echo all the way from the mountains to the valley. It was an especially hot and humid day. Shusuke was having a hard time falling asleep, so he stepped out of the house just under its eaves and sat alone on a rock, listening to the toads' croaking. He wiped away the tears that welled up as he reflected on the past years of his life and the frustration of not being able to improve the variation in the quality of the calves.

Whenever he found good quality cows, he bought them even though that meant he had to sell part of his family's fortune. He mixed breeding of this and that, but there was still none that could be a strain to become a vine of lineage. Even for the cowherd boy, the inconsistency of the cattle quality was an impenetrable issue to resolve, which shattered his confidence. He looked up at the full moon and muttered to himself.

"Where should I look to find a good cow that can be a vine of lineage? All of the cattle that I have now are good cattle, but the quality of their offspring is not always meeting the gold standard. It's not acceptable. How long do I have to do this….?"

Right then, Oyoshi came out of the house, bringing a cover-up for her husband.

"Hun, I don't want you to catch a cold. You need to watch out for the night dew, even in summer."

She wrapped it around his shoulders.

Her unexpected kindness stiffened his shoulders. He quickly shifted his face away from her so that she wouldn't notice him crying. Oyoshi chuckled.

"Well, you caught me in my weakened state," muttered Shusuke.

"Don't rush yourself. I knew it would be a lifelong project from the beginning. If you can produce a vine within a decade or so, then such work isn't worth much after all. But I do believe that somewhere under this sky, the 'Miraculous Cow' that you've been seeking is awaiting," said Oyoshi, wrapping her hands around Shusuke's cold hands and blowing on them to keep them warm.

"A miraculous cow......Oyoshi, "do you think there is really such a cow?"

"Hmm, it's not like you, Shusuke. Of course, there is a miraculous cow. Look, close your eyes and wish for a cow that you want over and over, and God will grant your wish."

The way she said it, as if there was nothing to be concerned about, encouraged him to regain the strength to keep trying to bring back his enthusiasm once more.

He stood up from the rock and looked up at the night sky with Oyoshi. The light of a magnificent full moon illuminated them both.

In Shusuke's backyard, several chickens walked around as if they owned the entire space. Sometimes, they went outside of the property, but chickweed and shepherd's purses were carefully selected to blend into the cattle feed. Finding nothing to munch on, the chickens gave up and came back in.

While it was still dim, the earliest bird began crowing. With that as an alarm, Shusuke began to wake up, and half an hour later, when the second earliest chicken crowed, it was time for him to get up and start his day. It was still sometime between 5 to 6 am.

This morning started the same when the earliest bird crowed as usual. However, it was followed by a commotion and the loud chirping of other chickens. Hearing that, Shusuke thought a dog might have come to disturb them, but if so, it normally caused a commotion in the cowshed as well.....As he was trying to figure it out, a man's loud voice came from outside.

"Shu, Shusuke, are you there?"

Someone was banging on the front door, making a rattling noise. Shusuke jumped out of his bed and opened the backyard window by his bed.

"What is it? Oh, Sasuke. What made you hurry?"

Sasuke stood under the dim sky, breathing hard. When he saw Shusuke's face, he bent his body into a crook and put his hands on his knees, trying to catch his breath. Lately, Sasuke had received compensation from Shusuke for his labor to help pull cattle for the cattle market.

"Sorry to wake you up so early in the morning, but it's an emergency."

After telling him so, Sasuke walked around to the yard next to the entrance, which made the chickens think something terrible had happened, so they jumped up and down with even more excitement.

"Shusuke, have you ever visited Muraoka village, our neighboring village? Rumor has it that there is a truly amazing cow there."

Intuitively, Shusuke reacted to Sasuke's words, "rumor" and "good cow."

"Great! I'm going there right now. Come with me."

Shusuke invited Sasuke into the entranceway and called out to the back of the house.

"Oyoshi! Oyoshiii!"

She was already awake and preparing breakfast.

"What's going on? You don't need to yell. I can hear you fine."

As she wiped her hands with a towel, she came out to the entrance and kneeled on the floor.

"Oh, hello, Sasuke. Thank you for always supporting my husband's work. Why don't you come on in and have breakfast with us?"

She welcomed Sasuke warmly. Sasuke wiped the sweat off his face with a towel wrapped around his neck and bashfully greeted her, "Hello, Oyoshi. You are always beautiful, and it's such a joy to see you."

Oyoshi laughed, "Oh, Sasuke, don't flatter me so." Her laughter made him happy and brightened his day. In fact, she was the most beautiful woman in the village and also a daughter of a wealthy family, like what we call a truly pure closeted maiden. Shusuke was also the most handsome man in the village, so naturally, they made the best couple.

"Oyoshi, would you prepare 10 servings of huge rice balls, 7 bottles of unfiltered Sake, and some sweet mochi for us? We are leaving to visit the neighboring village so don't have time for breakfast."

She replied, "Okay, I'm on it."

…. But why had he requested more rice balls than usual?.... She murmured while preparing the huge rice balls.

"Oyoshi, we are going to check out the good cow in Muraoka, taking into account the rumor. Please don't tell my father."

"Well, you are traveling to the neighboring village this time? I see. Honey, I pray for you that you can meet the miraculous cow," said Oyoshi. She wrapped their lunch in one cloth and put that seemingly heavy pile at the entrance.

Shusuke clenched his fists and answered back, "yeah," reassuringly.

"You shouldn't drink too much, okay? Sasuke, please watch him," asked Oyoshi.

"Oyoshi, thank you for your kindness," said Sasuke, scratching his head and bowing sincerely. They left Ojiro.

Shusuke headed for the upriver village, guided by Sasuke. Since they had departed without eating breakfast, their stomachs told them it was already time to eat lunch. Sitting side by side by the clear stream in the forest, they ate rice balls and drank sake as if they were on a picnic. Sasuke was a little tipsy with a slight blush on his cheeks and asked Shusuke, "Hey, Shusuke. What drives you so much to find good cows?"

Shusuke looked up at the sky and smiled as he gulped down a handful of rice ball. Seeing his profile, Sasuke felt a bracing feeling as though standing under the clear blue sky.

"What drives me? I don't know what it is either, but I can see it clearly. I can see the impressive cattle grazing freely on the wide slopes of the mountain, sold for top dollar at the market, and the smoke rising from the chimneys of the houses in this village as residents cook their supper. I can see it. No one should suffer, like poor little Ume, in the village anymore."

"You can see it….? I see. I really wish that would happen. Okay, let me support you more."

Lightly tapping on his knee, Sasuke also looked up at the sky as he heartily ate his rice ball. Shusuke declared that he could see it, which somehow made Sasuke feel as if he too had seen the same vision. It made him want to share Shusuke's passion together.

"Thank you, Sasuke. I know the true value of Tajima cattle very well. However, when it comes to producing good quality cattle consistently from generation to generation, it's not simple. Until we can establish that, it will take a lot of effort to grow one good vine."

They finally arrived in Muraoka in the afternoon. At a tea shop, while they enjoyed tea and mochi, Sasuke asked the tea shop owner, "Pop, we heard that there is a great cow in Muraoka, so we came down from Ojiro. Do you know anything about it?"

"A great cow? Maybe…Is that about the cow of Miyoshi Genzaemon, who lives alone in the mountains of …… Oshinden? Perhaps, you should visit him. I hear that he has a good cow that gives birth to females every year."

Sasuke and Shusuke looked at each other, smiled, and stood up at the same time.

"Thanks, Pop. It was good mochi. Here is the money."

"Thank you. Turn left on this street. It's not too far."

After a little walk, they found a house in the middle of nowhere. It was surrounded by a bamboo grove, making them a little hesitant to get closer. But they were determined and looked at each other, and Shusuke called out loudly to the front door.

"Is this Miyoshi Genzaemon's residence?"

A man who looked over 80 years old with his back slightly bent emerged from the cattle shed next to the entrance. He answered, "Yap. I'm here."

As the two men walked toward the shed, Genzaemon came out of it, wiping his sweat with a hand towel hanging around his neck.

"I'm Shusuke Maeda from Ojiro. Sorry to bother you in the middle of your work."

"Oh, well. You are…I heard that there is a Dai-bakuro at Ojiro. Your name is well known even in Muraoka village. Why don't you take a look at my cow? She is a really great cow."

Shusuke suppressed his excitement. What would he do if he had come this far, yet was disappointed…?

"What do you think?" Genzaemon called out to them from behind.

Sasuke turned and asked, "What about those calves, Genzaemon?"

Genzaemon explained, "Those are the three calves she gave birth to. This one's mother is that one. That one's calf is there. The mother cow always gives birth to the same kind of calves every year, only female calves. She has the perfect female birthing belly."

Proudly, Genzaemon introduced his cattle to the visitors. There, they had beautiful shiny black coats, standing quietly. Without a word, Shusuke observed them with a serious look in his eyes. He checked the knee angles of their hind legs, the tone of the muscles, the balance of the hips and front legs, and so on. Then, he approached the cows and gently stroked their noses. Probably they could tell Shusuke was an unparalleled cow lover. They were not even afraid to stick their faces out at him. Their soft bushy foreheads were astonishingly shiny, and their cute round eyes seemed to adore Shusuke. He'd already decided what he was going to do. He was determined to get them.

"Genzaemon, this is a wonderful cow. All her offspring look just like their mother, and her mother looks just like her, too. Even from different generations, they remain the same," commented Shusuke.

"Such an amazing cow comes along only once in a hundred years. ......" Sasuke chimed in, not to be outdone. "Even I can tell she's a good cow."

"Once in a hundred years? Is she that good?"

The old Genzaemon seemed excited as he placed his hand on his aching back. Shusuke quickly replied,

"I've been registering every cattle in my village for years, so I can tell what is really good. I love her. Let me buy this cow, her mother, her calf, and all of her offspring, for the price you call. How about 20 ryo? No, wait, 30 ryo? Please let me buy them, I beg you."

Genzaemon was stunned by the unexpectedly large sum of money.

"Really? That's very generous of you. I'm getting old, so I was thinking that I would be very grateful if you would buy my cattle from me. With that much money, I could live the rest of my life without any worries."

"It's me, who should thank you. It's all I could have hoped for."

On the way home after he received the four cows, he suddenly stopped and began to weep profusely. Sasuke looked at Shusuke who was crying tears of joy. Concerned, he asked, "Shusuke, how are you going to come up with 30 ryo? It's a big number."

Shusuke replied, not even bothering to wipe away his tears. "I'll manage, somehow. ...... Well, it's not as if I have enough money or some way to cover the cost just now. But look, Sasuke. I finally found a cow that can become a vine of lineage. It took me fifteen years, but now I'm almost there. I couldn't be any happier. Thank you, Sasuke, for finding it. Thank you very much."

Then, he muttered in a lower voice. "Oyoshi, we did it. We found the miraculous cow!"

His steps were light on the way home. Rubbing their necks made the miraculous cows happy, and they gratefully followed Shusuke and Sasuke. Before going home, they visited Katujiro Kurono, who was the husband of Shusuke's sister. Dawn arrives early in between the mountains.

"Good evening, sis."

When Shusuke called her out at the entrance of their house, his sister was in the middle of preparing dinner and peeked out from the entranceway. There were several cattle lined up outside of their entrance.

"What's the matter, Shusuke? Why are you pulling so many cows now?" she asked.

"Is Katsujiro here?"

Katsujiro must have heard him, and popped out of the back room, and said, "Well, come on in, Sasuke, you too. Have you had dinner yet? Let's have dinner together." inviting them in. Shusuke, Sasuke, Katsujiro, and Shusuke's sister sat around the hearth, and Shusuke drank all the Nigori Sake that he brought in.

"Katujito, I finally found a cow that can be a vine of lineage at Muraoka. Please take a look."

Shusuke then sat up to show Katsujiro the cows tied to stakes outside the entrance. His sister attempted to stop them, "Oh, come on, you guys can check the cows after dinner, can't you?"

"Sis, just for a minute. I need to show him first because, after dark, it's hard to check on black cows," said Shusuke, and they ran out to the front door, laughing.

"Wow, they all look exactly alike," said Katsujiro, quite astonished to see the four identical cows eating straw. Having no choice, she briskly came out to the front door as well and stated, "To me, all cattle that everyone owns look the same with black coats. I have no idea how they are identical or different. Can you guys tell them apart?"

Katsujiro turned around and spouted, "Once you become familiar with them, you'll recognize each of them. They all are indeed black with two eyes, one nose, and one mouth, but just as we can tell ourselves apart, you'll see that not all cows are the same."

"Yes, that's right Katsujiro," said Shusuke, "but now, finally our long journey in search of vines is over. Would you lend me some money?"

Katsujiro replied, "I know that you are different from other brokers. I believe in you. Rather, I'd actually bet on your dreams." To his hasty comment, his wife rolled her eyes and was about to go inside the house, but Katsujiro called her out from behind, "Hey, bring me my large wallet from over there, will you?"

"Okay, okay," she reluctantly answered. She wasn't too thrilled about that idea but brought back his cloth wallet from the next room anyways. Katsujiro untied the wallet and placed it on the wooden floor of the entranceway.

"Well, I've got only five ryo of gold, two kans of silver, and 750 monme, but I hope this will help you."

Saying so, he seemed a little disappointed, perhaps because he had expected to find a little more in his wallet. Shusuke thanked him repeatedly. Sasuke watched them with a smile on his face the whole time.

When both were full and tipsy, they returned to the Maeda house located a little further up on the hill. They tied up the four cows in the shed, and then Sasuke went back to his own home.

It was already midnight, so Shusuke decided to go to bed dressed as he was.

The next morning, he woke Oyoshi up to show her the cows from Muraoka village. Though she was not as good as Shusuke, over the course of taking care of cattle for years accustomed her eyes to being able to recognize each cow's face and evaluate their appearances. Rubbing her sleepy eyes, she saw the four almost identical cows and rubbed her eyes some more.

"Oyoshi, you are not in a dream."

She stepped closer to the cows and burst into tears.

"Shu, Shusuke…You've finally met the miraculous cow!"

They took each other's hands and hugged tightly as partners who shared the same hardships.

Chapter 9

Encounter with Bandits

Although the Maeda family had given up their mountain territory and was now burdened with a large amount of debt, Shusuke was just one step away from achieving his big dream of establishing a cattle business. Oyoshi was itching to contribute to his lifelong dream and wanted to do something more tangible.

Without telling Shusuke, Oyoshi was sorting through her Kimono chest of drawers to bring in her brand-new--not even taken the basting stitches off yet—best ceremonial kimono, five merceries, and a tortoiseshell comb to pawn shops, all of which were part of her wedding gifts. Unexpectedly, Shusuke's father, Izaemon walked in and found her pulling them out from her drawers. Immediately, he rushed to the cowshed to find his son. He grabbed Shusuke by his neck and threw a fist at him, yelling "You are such a moron!" Frightened, the cows started mooing in panic. Noticing the commotion in the cowshed, Oyoshi quickly went to the cowshed and saw Shusuke's old mother hanging on to Izaemon and pleading with him to stop.

Oyoshi realized that Izaemon had realized what she was about to do. She pleaded, "Oh, Izaemon, please don't be mad at him. It was me who decided to do what I was about to do. Shusuke has nothing to do with it."

"No, I can't let you be involved in the trouble that my son caused. He won't grow out of his cow hobby if I do so."

Izaemon bit his lip in disgust.

"Please excuse me for correcting you, but I must tell you that it is not just his hobby."

Before she could continue, Izaemon questioned Shusuke. "You leave the care of the cows to Oyoshi and still wander around all day long, don't you? And every time you go somewhere, you buy a new cow, is that right?"

And then, he dropped his fist, trembling with anger, onto Shusuke. Shusuke allowed himself to be beaten. Oyoshi covered Shusuke's body and said, "Izaemon, please stop now. Shusuke has finally discovered a cow that can become a vine. This is the last one, this is it."

Because of her words, Izaemon paused and pulled his hands away. Shusuke's mother was crying, not knowing what to do.

"Fine. Do whatever you want. But as I have warned you many times, don't bring shame to our relatives."

With that, Izaemon turned his back and headed toward the house, but when he opened the front door, he turned around with a downcast look on his face.

"Well, Shusuke. Congratulations. Oyoshi, thank you for your support."

He awkwardly mumbled in a low voice and walked into the house with his head hanging down.

"He found out I was scheming for money. I'm sorry that I put you in trouble."

She wiped the blood off at the edge of his mouth with a towel and helped him get up.

"I apologize that I troubled you, too. I'm sorry," said Shusuke.

"Honey, I really want to help you by any means. I don't need those kimonos as they were only just collecting dust in the drawer."

"Oh, Oyoshi. I'm so sorry. Please forgive him," Shusuke's mother apologized as she seemed to shrink even more. Oyoshi thought that she was the one making his mother feel miserable.

"No, no, mother, please," she apologized to her back in a tearful voice. Shusuke looked around at the cows, murmured, "It will be soon. ......," and clenched his fists so hard that his palms turned white.

Oyoshi thought the money she could obtain wouldn't be enough, so she visited her parents' house. Oyoshi's mother was sewing on the porch. As she put her luggage on the porch, her mother opened her mouth in search of words but just shook her head.

"Everyone in this village is talking about Shusuke and his work. Your father said that he would give out our entire warehouse to Shusuke, but it's not as if we can actually spare any extra money. So here, take this with you before your father finds it. I stashed some goods of value from the warehouse in it. And this one is a Saga Nishiki Obi belt. It is a work of art and should be valued at a very high price. Well, in case one day, this might happen, I gathered them all together in the corner there."

"Thank you, Mother. Shusuke is a man who makes things happen for everyone. I have a faith in him."

"I can understand how you feel about him and his dream, but you need to keep in mind that before you help others, you have to be able to feed yourself first."

Despite her complaints, her mother's profile resembled a gentle Buddha. When seeing her mother's profile, Oyoshi appreciated her and clasped her hands together in her mind.

Oyoshi came back with a handful of large sacks and baggage picked up from her parents' house. First, she put them in storage, and then she started putting on makeup in front of the mirror. To begin with, she was the most beautiful woman in the village, so with proper makeup, no one would think she was from a county village. After putting on her makeup, she changed into a ceremonial kimono. Once again, she quickly touched up in front of the mirror and headed over to the storage.

As she lifted all the luggage, her brother-in-law, Katsujiro came running breathlessly. "Phew, I made it just in time. You're dressing up and carrying heavy luggage…. Let me help you."

"How did you find out, Katsujiro?"

"Your mom told me. I thought you were plotting something like this anyway. Why didn't you tell me? Oyoshi, you don't have to do such a thing."

Katsujiro tried to pick up Oyoshi's baggage, but Oyoshi pulled it away from him and said, "You do things like pulling the cows, taking care of them, or even lending some money to Shusuke. I want to contribute somehow, too. I'm tired of being just a bystander."

"Well, I guess I can't stop you. Then, let me come with you to the town."

"That's great. I can surely count on you. Thank you so much."

Katsujiro carried her baggage on his back and started a small conversation to hear her thoughts.

"You've been through a lot, haven't you?"

"People often say that to me, but I actually find it amusing. It's much more interesting than a life with nothing at all. I was hoping to meet someone like that."

Oyoshi's face was as radiant as the sky today, and her eyes were shining. Katsujiro looked at her and thought she was probably more beautiful than any woman in any village.

"You're right. It is very interesting. It's the same for me too. I also find it amusing," Katsujiro said.

They both laughed heartily. Suddenly, the bamboo on the side of the road made a rustling sound. The sound was moving from place to place.

"Shush. Oyoshi, don't move."

Just then, several raccoons ran out of the bamboo grove, rapidly crossed in front of them, and disappeared into the bamboo grove on the other side. The two were a little startled, but when they realized that it was just raccoons making that sound, they felt relieved and resumed walking again. However, a deep voice came behind them and stopped them once again.

"Hey, there. Leave your baggage or else…."

It was a bandit. A giant man with a beard and wearing a bear fur coat was standing there.

"Oyoshi, run!"

As Oyoshi started to run, the bamboo branches made a rustling sound, and four men emerged to block her way, gradually closing in on her from all sides. All four men were carrying branches over their shoulders. A perfect branch lay in front of Katsujiro, so he picked it up without taking his eyes off them.

Katsujiro retreated while protecting Oyoshi.

"I've mastered   Yagyu Shinkage-Ryu. Are you sure you want to challenge me?"

Katsujiro held up the branch. His posture and eagle-eye told the bandits that he was a highly skilled swordsman. The two men on either side simultaneously jumped at Katsujiro, yet he quickly stabbed one in the stomach with the stick and bashed the other one's arm making him crop the branch from his hand. Oyoshi came behind Katsujiro, glaring at the bandits. Witnessing this, the other two flinched a little. "Eeeeek!" Oyoshi screamed as she chucked stones in all directions.

"I can't run away either. My future depends on this trip!"

"Ouch! You bitch!"

One of the bandits attacked Oyoshi from behind and lifted her up on his shoulder.

"Noooo! Let go of me!"

Lifted up by surprise, Oyoshi was startled and kicked her legs in the air struggling to escape.

"Damn it! Let go of her! Here, I'll leave our baggage, but let go of her."

Katsujiro placed their baggage down by his feet.

Still captured, Oyoshi shouted, "I need to sell these so we can pay off Shusuke's cows. I won't let you have them."

"Hold on, Shusuke? Are you Brother Shusuke Maeda's wife, by any chance?" The bandit wearing the fur coat asked Oyoshi.

"Y…, yes, I am."

Hearing her answer, he glared at the others and ordered, "Hey, you guys. Drop it. Don't be disrespectful. She is Brother Shusuke Maeda's wife."

Hastily, the young bandit carefully put her down on the ground and asked her if she was hurt, apologizing over and over. The man in his thirties wearing the fur coat seemed to be the leader of this bandit group. On the other hand, Oyoshi and Katsujiro couldn't understand what had just happened,   so they stood there in a daze.

The attitude of the man in the fur coat dramatically changed and he knelt down and begged for forgiveness. "We are sorry," apologized the bandit. Then the other four followed him as well.

The man in the fur coat lifted his face up to see Oyoshi and said, "We are so sorry. How terrible of what we did to you. My name is Sukezo. Mr. Shusuke looks after us very well. A while ago, we did the same thing to him as well. We stopped him on his way to rob him also."

He began to talk about how he knew Shusuke. Katsujiro and Oyoshi were relieved and sat down on a nearby stump. Sukezo and the other young bandits sat down cross-legged. The story that Sukezo told went like this.

One day, Shusuke was passing the mountain road with two cows. Suddenly, a group of five bandits silently appeared in front of him, carrying thick branches on their shoulders, puffing and panting.

"Well, I have cows but don't have any money before selling them, so you are just wasting your time," said Shusuke with a soft smile on his face.

Sukezo demanded, "Then, give up your cows."

Shusuke replied, "Okay, that's fine, but these cows only listen to me. You can't make them move no matter how hard you try even by hitting them. Go ahead, try it."

The young one attempted to pull the reins, but the cow would not budge at all. The sight amused Shusuke for a while. Then, all of the sudden, Shusuke began untying the baggage that was hanging on the cow's back.

"Before that, I've got some rice balls and unfiltered sake," he said. "I'm getting hungry. Why don't you guys have some lunch with me?"

In the baggage, there were ten huge rice balls and seven bamboo bottles containing unfiltered sake. As they saw Shusuke pulling food and drinks out, the bandits looked at each other, not knowing what to do.

Shusuke urged the bandits, "Come on, it's a party. Here, eat up. Help yourself. Nothing is better than Oyoshi's rice ball."

Shusuke handed Sukezo a rice ball first. Sukezo looked puzzled but took a bite.

"Ummm. It's so good." Instantly, he gobbled up more.

"Right? A big Kishu plum is inside. Here, eat up, young man. I have some unfiltered sake, too. Oyoshi made it as well. Oh, and I also have some good sweet mochi today."

With his head, Sukezo signaled his friends to eat as well. All six of them sat down in a circle. Shusuke fed the cows, which were tied to a nearby tree. What made Shusuke happy was enjoying a picnic under the blue sky with people, drinking unfiltered sake. That was the reason why he always asked Oyoshi to make him extra rice balls. She didn't know why, so she just thought, "oh my, he must have such a big appetite."

"By the way, what are you guys doing here?"

The bandits, who had been silently stuffing their mouths, were startled by his question. A young man patted Sukezo on his back as he was choking on his food.

"What are we doing here? Isn't it obvious? We are bandits."

"Oh, yeah. Right. Why are you guys doing such a thing?"

"Because we want money, why else?"

"Humm, I see. ....understandable. You cannot help it if you can't feed yourself. Well, drink up."

Shusuke offered the sake to the five men.

"Wow. This sake is really good. Hey, you guys should try it. I haven't had such good sake in years."

Feeling a little tipsy, Shusuke asked the same question again, "So, why are you all doing this?"

"We were orphans. Since we were little, we have been stealing potatoes or something to eat from our neighbors...... I don't know how I survived until now, but come to think of it, I think those farmers let us off the hook. I don't know how I became an orphan. This is how our people have lived since we were small."

Shusuke was very susceptible to this kind of story.

"Eat these mochis, too," and Shusuke passed sweet mochi to them.

"Do you guys have any dreams?"

"All we can do is to find food to eat day after day. We can't afford to have a dream," said one of the young men.

At his words, another young man said, "Wait a minute. My dream has come true. I've always wanted to eat rice balls till I can eat no more, but here I am. Not only that, but I can enjoy good sake and sweet mochi, too."

"You're right," said Sukezo, laughing so much. The young man who said it was smiling embarrassedly.

"What a wonderful day. I'm having the time of my life."

For the first time in a long time, they smiled carefreely. Shusuke loved to see people smile as much as he loved cows.

Stuffed and satisfied, Sukezo asked Shusuke in return. "Sorry that we'd been talking so much about us. What about you? What is your name? Do you have a dream?" Now, he was interested in Shusuke.

"Me? My name is Shusuke Maeda."

"Shusuke, Maeda….hmm. I think I've heard about you somewhere. Perhaps, at the foot of the mountain, some cow brokers were talking about you…. Oh, I see, you are that Shusuke Maeda."

"I know, you've probably heard unfavorable rumors about me, haven`t you? Like, I'm a cow hoarder, a fool, and so on," said Shusuke.

"Well, I don't deny that some rumors are unfriendly," laughed Sukezo.

"That's fine. I don't mind. I am a big fool. But, you know what, I have a dream."

"Hmm. What is it?" The young bandits leaned forward, too.

"I'm going to make the people of this valley rich. My dream is to make this valley the best cattle ranch in Japan. People will recognize Ojiro for Tajima cattle."

Shusuke stared at the wide valley far in his sight.

"Now I know. You are truly a big fool. We are also from Ojiro. Are you going to make us rich, too?"

It was a gamble for Sukezo.

"Of course. My dream is to make you guys able to feed yourself without having to do all these things and marry someone you'll love."

"Marry someone……. that would be such a wonderful future to look forward to." The fellow bandits eagerly nodded at each other.

"So, what should we do? Money is good, but we want to do something meaningful."

"Well, that doesn't sound like bandits."

"We still have a lot of stamina. We would be grateful if there were some other jobs that we could be useful for, but people avoid eye contact with someone like us. They won't even let us help them with their work." Sukezo sighed.

"Then, I have something for you guys to do. For now, brush these cows with straw to make their fur shiny and glossy. Later on, I'll bring more cows, and I want you guys to brush them each time. The final finishing touch is very important before I send them to the market."

"All right. Get in pairs and start polishing those cows now. And you go fetch water," Sukezo ordered his men, and they began to move briskly. Shusuke drank his sake smiling and looking up at the sky.

When Sukezo finished polishing the cows, he proudly presented the shiny black cows to Shusuke and asked, "What do you think, brother Shusuke?" The cows seemed to enjoy the brush treatment, narrowing their eyes.

Shusuke was quite impressed with their work but suddenly asked, "By the way, what is 'brother' supposed to mean?"

"You are like my brother. Sorry, if I'm too overfamiliar."

"Sure, sure. But, my goodness, they look so much better. It's a lot quicker and better than I do it by myself. Thank you. Now, I'm going to sell them at the market, so I will pay you some money for your labor." Shusuke hoped to have a chance to meet them again.

For the bandits, it was the first time ever in their lives that someone appreciated and praised them for their work. The five grinned at each other, embarrassed, but their feelings were brighter than the sky.

"No, no, no. We ate so much food, so we need to get moving."

Perhaps even Sukezo felt embarrassed by working earnestly, and he made an awkward excuse.

"I'll go through this pass again, so please help me out when I do. I'll bring lunch that Oyoshi makes to share with you. And then, later on, I'll ask you to come down to Ojiro village, so please join us and help me."

"Will you let us take part in your dream of a big ranch?" asked Sukezo, and other young bandits shook their heads in agreement. Their grim eyes were now filled with a glimmer of hope and vigor.

"Really? That's awesome! You are going to support this fool's dream?" Shusuke asked.

To his word, one of the young bandits responded, "Of..., of course. We are just like *Momotaro's retainers."

By his comment, everyone burst into laughter.

"That's great!" Shusuke also let out a belly laugh."

"...and that's how we met him." Sukezo finished his story.

It was not much of a surprise for Oyoshi to imagine how he would be.

"Right. Brother Shusuke listened to us, and that's what made me happy the most. Nobody even cares to listen to what we want to say....." One of the young men said, and the others nodded their vigorous agreement.

"It totally sounds like him to do such a thing. Now I know why he needed that many rice balls and sake to bring along," said Katsujiro with a wry smile, but he was very proud of Shusuke in his heart.

"Thank you for preparing food for us, too, every time he passes through this way, and sorry for making you work extra for us. But we truly admire his passion." Sukezo said with a serious face.

*Momotaro or "Peach Boy" is a hero in well-known Japanese folklore. Animals followed him to defeat demons in return for the sweet mochi that he gave them.

Oyoshi said, "You guys should never do anything that will cause trouble for others again. If you keep doing that, it will deeply hurt my husband's feelings. You know what, he will be very busy from now on, so please come down from the mountain in the middle of the month to visit us. There will be plenty of job opportunities for you," bowing to them.

"We are sorry. We did it again, not considering how Brother Shusuke feels. From now on, we want to mend our ways and help him out."

Sukezo wiped away his tears. "Okay, you guys. Carry that baggage over the mountain for them and use your manners," ordered Sukezo.

His men carried baggage that Katsujiro held on his back, while Sukezo and another man carried Oyoshi on a straw mat.

"This is so nice," said Oyoshi.

"Oyoshi, it looks like Shusuke got you again."

The smiles on their faces were a tribute to Shusuke's character.

Chapter 10

Oyoshi's Momentous Decision

After Oyoshi exchanged farewells with the men at the foot of the mountain and later parted from Katsujiro in Osaka, she headed for Imabashi in Osaka, alone. Crowds of people were streaming around in the bustling town. A mother with her little girl who was pleading for a windmill, a man wearing a hat on his close-cropped head, and so on. Everything that she saw astonished her. As she walked through the town, she found a bright red sign at the end of the main street. Just the word "Pawn" was written on it in large letters without the name of the store.

A man came out of the shop. Although he was well-dressed, as he walked out, he looked around nervously and quickly walked away. Oyoshi was a little embarrassed to see herself in her best kimono. It seemed that everyone thought the same way: no one wanted others to think they came to the pawnshop because they had fallen into poverty, so they dressed up the best they could. Perhaps, the pawnshop owner knew that as well. Anyway, it was too late to make any changes now. So Oyoshi let out a sigh and stepped through the doorway.

The pawnshop owner waited on her with his eyes downcast. Probably, it was his way to be polite to his customers by avoiding facing them directly. Oyoshi unfolded her baggage in front of the owner.

For the first time, he looked up and saw her face, moving his gaze back and forth between her face and the goods. "Oh my.... These are very fine pieces. It's not so easy to find such fine quality. Hmm, this one is a Kyoyuzen Obi belt, and that one is a Saga Nishiki Obi belt, aren't they? What wonderful quality. I can easily sell these well-crafted materials to gentlemen who are regulars in the red-light district. Wow, this scroll is another beautiful piece. ......"

The owner seemed quite impressed with each item as he evaluated them one by one. He seemed curious about what kind of person would bring such items to a pawn shop and for what reason.

"Well then, could you please buy them at the highest price you can?"

"Okay, let me see what I can do for you. But you know, I am running a business here, so how about this much? It's my best offer."

Oyoshi moved one ball on his abacus and pleaded, "I implore you, this much…"

The owner patted his thinning forehead. "Hmm, well. You've got me. You must have a compelling reason. All right, done. I'll pay," agreed the owner.

"Thank you so much. Do you know anywhere that I can deposit this money?"

"Osaka's top money exchangers gather in this area, so if you walk straight down the street in front of this shop, you will find Echigo-ya, a money changer, or turn around that corner, you will find Kashima-ya. There are about five other shops as well. Lately, their main customers are former Samurais lending some money, so they'll be happy to accept your deposit."

"Thank you, I appreciate your kindness."

When Oyoshi was about to leave the store, the owner stopped her for a moment.

"I'm not supposed to ask any questions to my customers….but I hope you don't mind if I ask you a personal question. What's going on?"

Oyoshi smiled a little and replied. "I'm helping to support my husband's dream. A dream to bring prosperity to our village ……. I was drawn in by his big dream of making our poor village the best in Japan. It made me feel like doing something that I didn't have to do."

Upon hearing her answer, he put an additional three *bu in Oyoshi's hand.

"What's this?" asked Oyoshi.

---

* "Bu" was Old Japanese currency. A quarter of Ryo, which was a larger currency.

"Let me help you and your husband's dream. You know, in my business, I've been dealing with despondent people, which made me depressed, too. Your dream brightened my day for the first time in a while."

Oyoshi bowed low to him.

After leaving the pawnshop and walking a little further, she found a navy-blue sign that read "Echigo-ya, the money changer." Next to the Echigo-ya store was probably the residence of the owner. A large branch of a cherry tree was spreading over the path of the bamboo fence surrounding the mansion. Despite the occasional gusts of wind, the dark pink petals of the double-flowered cherry blossoms were clinging to the branch and showed no sign of falling off. The sight braced her up.

Before entering the premises, she put on her best *haori coverup and checked her appearance with a handheld mirror. When she confidently stepped inside the shop, the manager's eye was caught by her beautiful rich lady-like appearance. He hurried out from his podium to greet her in person, kneeling down with a smile on his face.

"Greetings, madam. How may I assist you today?"

"My wallet is a little too heavy to carry around. I'd like to ask you to keep my money for a little while…."

"Of course, I am more than happy to assist you with that. We appreciate your business."

"Thank you. I'm visiting a nearby shop, but I am not comfortable carrying money with me. May I please have a certificate of deposit?"

As she carefully asked, she pulled out seven ryo and three bu of the money from her sleeve. The manager properly counted the money and issued a receipt.

"Madam, please come back again and deposit with us," said he, bowing graciously.

*Haori: Japanese traditional cover-up or Kimono Jacket

After spending a few hours wandering here and there, Oyoshi returned to Echigo-ya.

Then, she asked, "I have some business to take care of...... May I withdraw the money I just deposited earlier?"

"Have you already finished what you need to do? That's great. You're more than welcome to come back any time. May I have your certificate of deposit?"

It was the first time for Oyoshi to act her socks off ever in her lifetime.

"Let me see...Oh, dear. I am certain that I've put it in my sleeve. ......Oh, my goodness, I can't find it."

From the moment he first saw her, the manager had trusted Oyoshi who seemed innocent and trustworthy, so he just said, "Well, no worries. If you find it, tear it up and dispose of it. I will write a receipt to prove that I returned the money, and all I need from you is your signature on the receipt."

He counted the money, confirming "Here is the total amount that I've gotten from you, correct?" and returned the bag to Oyoshi.

As soon as she walked out of the shop, she then went into a money changer called Yoshida-ya a few doors down on the right. This time, she spoke to the manager first.

"Hello. Isn't it a beautiful day today? I would like to deposit some money...."

She spoke briefly in an accustomed manner. The rhythmical sound of the abacus immediately stopped, and the manager came out to the front to assist her.

"Yes, indeed, but it is rather too hot for me. You don't look familiar. Where are you from?" He said smiling amiably. Oyoshi flinched a little, thinking that it was obvious to him that she was from a country village, but she once again inserted her hairpin deeply into her hair and replied with confidence.

"I'm from the countryside of Tajima. My sleeves are heavy because of the money from the sale of the cows." Her answer showed no hesitation.

"Hmm…Tajima cows. I have heard rumors about them recently. They produce very fine quality cows. I heard that no matter how much you pay for Tajima cows, you can sell them for even higher prices. One of the cow brokers that I know lamented that he wanted to buy more, but their shrewd broker, whose name is Shusuke Maeda, holds back the cows."

Oyoshi was surprised. It was the first time she directly heard about Tajima cows and Shusuke, and not only that, it was from someone in a different field of business in Osaka. She chuckled.

"That Shusuke is my husband. Do you hear that Tajima cows are really appraised that good?"

To her words, the manager was dismayed, hiding his reddened forehead with his palm. "Oh, pardon me. He is? My apologies. I didn't know you are his wife. Oh well…What I hear from many brokers is that your husband's cows are currently invincible and have the market all to themselves. I would like to see his Tajima cows for myself one of these days. People say that even though Tajima cows are brought from far away, they don't get exhausted."

"I see. He hasn't brought in any of his truly favorite cows to the market yet…."

"Uh, that's what the other brokers were talking about. He has so many great cows back in his village, but he has no intention of bringing them into the market."

Oyoshi cleared her throat.

"Oh, I'm sorry, I've been chatting too long. Lately, there isn't much exciting news, so I was just…," he trailed off.

She took her money bag out of her sleeve and handed it to the manager. He began counting, muttering to himself, "Impressive."

Oyoshi asked him, "May I have the certificate of deposit?"

"Certainly. How would you like to be paid the interest?" The manager asked.

"I'm just going shopping around nearby stores for a little while, so that won't be necessary. I'm not comfortable carrying around a large sum of money with me…I'll be back soon."

"I understand. Enjoy shopping."

"Thank you so much for your information, Sir."

With that, she left the shop and went out to the main street. She put the certificate away in her sleeve and clenched her fist with excitement.

---Shusuke is right. Ojiro valley will be saved, no doubt about it.

Convinced by the fact, her cheeks turned even brighter than cherry blossoms.

After that, she repeated the same scheme at three more money changers and received a certificate of deposit each time. At last, she entered Tennoji-ya, the largest money changer in Osaka. The store was crowded with people.

Their manager approached her as if drawn by Oyoshi's beautiful smile. Oyoshi showed him some cash and five certificates pulled out from her sleeve.

"I came from Tajima. I have been depositing the same amount of money here and there every time a cow is sold, but since I need to buy a stud bull, could you lend me some money keeping these as collateral? I'm getting tired of walking around to all the places where I deposited the money."

The manager looked at the substantial amount of money written on the certificate of deposits.

"Well, if you have collateral, we are more than happy to help you with your business. You seem to be very well off in this tough time, ma'am."

His comment made Oyoshi slightly afraid that he might have noticed something, but she put on an impassive act here as well.

"Oh? Do you think the recent economy is that bad? Well then, we are blessed to have a large number of high-quality cattle. Cows are gods to us," she said.

"That is really good for you, ma'am. Sure, I hear about the Tajima cows even all the way here in Osaka. People call them 'rare cattle that you can seldom see.' Oh, yeah. Tajima black cattle were used to build the stone walls of Osaka Castle there. They were docile and obedient to people. I see, I see. I will lend you as much as you wish. But in return, please patronize us again, ma'am."

Chapter 11

The Cow brokers at the Mountain Pass

The following evening, Oyoshi returned home very exhausted. She handed Shusuke forty ryo, a very large sum of money. He was extremely surprised.

"Wow, this is amazing. How did you collect such a large amount of money? You know what, Oyoshi? With this much money, we could buy ten more cows of good quality."

"Honey, from now on, I need you to sell whenever a good calf is born as often as you can. I borrowed this money from the money exchanger, so we have to make sure to pay them back by the due date," told Oyoshi.

Shusuke replied, "Okay, I'll do that. I've come to understand the rule of sums about cows by now. I learned that a good calf is born more efficiently to a good female cow than to a good male, and that's a big step forward. Besides, Genzaemon's miracle cows give birth every year to female calves that look just like their mothers. We have three of them, which means a multiple of three."

Looking at the money, he was as excited as a child.

"In Osaka, I heard rumors about you and the Tajima cows," said Oyoshi.

"Really? It was probably people talking nonsense about me, wasn't it?"

Oyoshi chuckled at his words and waved her hand from side to side.

"No, no. They said that Tajima cows are tough and full of stamina and they never get tired, with shiny black coats that they've never seen anywhere else. They can be easily sold quickly and at the highest price ever, but the brokers lamented that the shrewd broker, whose name is Maeda, rarely brings them into the market even though they are in high demand."

Shusuke shook her shoulder, wearing a big smile on his face as he repeated,

"Is that so? Is that really so? You heard people saying so, Oyoshi?"

Oyoshi smiled back at him but before she could say anything, slumped down exhausted. He tucked her into the blanket and gazed at her sleeping face as he lay by her side.

"Thank you. Thank you very much, Oyoshi. Katsujiro told me a little bit about what you were doing. I'm sorry I put you through so much hardship. We are almost there. After Genzaemon's cows give birth to the new calves, I will lend them to the entire village for breeding first. Then, the next generation will be born. Once it succeeds, then the creating vine of linage will be complete."

Oyoshi was fast asleep, deeply enough to snore, so Shusuke's voice did not reach her ears.

The following day, Shuseke gathered his relatives.

"First, I'd like to apologize to Oyoshi's father and Oyoshi. Also, I am truly sorry for borrowing money from all my relatives, but not only that, asking you to take care of the cows. But now, I am ready to settle. I've completed a survey of all the cows in this village and learned where each calf was born, from which parents, and how they were raised. In just one month, all the cows in this village will start calving. Please bear with me for the next six months. Moreover, in the village of Muraoka, I found good cows that can create a sustainable vine. I was expecting to have to wait for a long while until we could keep producing good quality cows constantly, but now I can tell that we are on right track to save our village."

Shusuke reported along with his greeting. Fifteen years had passed since he had decided to save the village with cows.

Izaemon added, "We really appreciate all of you, and we want to apologize for getting you all involved in this fool's plan." With his sincere words, Izaemon bowed his head lower.

Right then, they heard someone calling out in the backyard. "Brother Shusuke!" It was the five former bandits. Izaemon and the relatives were stunned by the sight of these shaggy unfamiliar-looking men.

Shusuke went to the porch leading to their backyard and greeted, "Hi there, thank you all very much for coming. Starting tomorrow, we will be busy, so I'm counting on you guys. Oyoshi will teach you everything from how to choose the proper feed to how to raise cattle. Also, we're going to bring out more cows than before, so we'll need more hands. I'd very much appreciate it if you can help us out with that, too. Oh, and then, I'm sorry to ask you this, but there is an extra cowshed that can be remodeled and cleaned for you guys to stay in until you can afford to start a family. You are more than welcome to join us for daily meals."

"Brother Shusuke…." Sukezo burst into tears and held Shusuke's hand.

Shusuke said, "Sure, sure. I really appreciate your help. If everyone can live happily together like this, that's all that matters to me."

Everyone, including Shusuke's parents and relatives, watched their conversation held on the porch in amazement. Katsujiro and Oyoshi looked at each other and laughed. However, since she was now in charge of preparing meals for the residents as well, her workload had drastically increased.

One day, Shusuke and the five former bandits were pulling six cows that villagers entrusted to them, to the market. However, when they reached the mountain pass, a bunch of cow brokers was waiting for them. Shusuke flinched slightly.

"What is going on? What are you guys doing here?"

"Shusuke, please let me buy this cow on your left. I have four ryo here. Take it."

Before he could say anything, one of them put a price on it. Then, another one protested,

"Hey, hold on! I was here before you. You have no right to call it first."

Then, another man also yelled, "Come on! I was here before those two. If this is first come first serve, then it should be me who's at the priority!"

"Nonsense! The highest bidder gets it first, it's common sense!"

"Are you kidding? Then, I go first!"

--The situation got out of control, and eventually, a big fight broke out. Shusuke couldn't bear to see it, so he interrupted.

"Hold on, you guys. No need to fight. For this time, I'll sell them for four ryo in the order of those who came waiting early. But next time, I will sell them to the one who bids the highest price."

With his words, all six cows were sold at the mountain pass.

Ever since then, the "auction" ambushes kept recurring at the mountain pass. Each time, the cattle were sold like hot cakes at a high price of five or six ryo, and eventually, there were no more cows left to sell at the market. As Shusuke had hoped, Ojiro and Muraoka became well known for their quality cattle, and the quality of life of the villagers became better.

Eventually, all of the bandits found the love of their lives, married, and settled in the village. Occasionally bandit-like newcomers from elsewhere entered the village, but Sukezo heard them out and found them suitable jobs. In this way, Sukezo eventually became a coordinator in the village. In the nearby mountains, the villagers took care of cattle grazing with love and affection.

Cattle lovers and brokers gathered at Shusuke's house all the time, and they discussed cattle for a while. Oyoshi was as busy as a bee, taking care of their guests by preparing their meals and so on, but it didn't wear her out nor pain her at all. She was grateful to have people gathered around with love and respect.

Once, people used to talk behind his back, calling him names like "A cow crazy Shusuke Maeda," but who knew? Now, it turned out that more and more people gathered around Shusuke. Occasionally, Oyoshi had to stay up late to make pillows out of the comforters for their extra guests. People visited the cowshed more frequently, and some even paid for the calves on the spot as soon as they were born.

In the Maeda family's backyard, small red Japanese quince flowers were in full bloom, under which stalks of chickweeds were stretching their stems, and chickens were pecking at them impatiently with their beaks as if they were afraid that Shusuke would pick them all to feed his cows.

A town express messenger passed by and called out, "Hi, Mr. Maeda. Which cow are you planning to sell this time?"

"The second one from the left. Also, the one at Sasuke's house…and…. yap. We have ten great calves that have been born in our village, so I have to take them to the market. I'll be busy soon."

"But lately, the brokers come to you even before you go to the market, don't they?"

"Yeah. Look, so many of them are already here today, even though we don't have enough seats for them. Everyone loves cows, so they enjoy having a long talk about cows. I guess they're trying to find out what they're looking for while they're here."

Shusuke answered with a proud smile on his face.

"Sounds about right. It must be very busy for Oyoshi to serve them drinks all day long. You should make sure she doesn't overwork herself and watch out for her health."

"Thank you," he said. "Oyoshi likes to have many people around, so she also enjoys having guests."

"No, no. I think that it's quite tiring to be a host. Here, this letter is for you. I'm still in the middle of my work, so I'll talk to you later."

Shusuke received his letter at the door and sat down on the porch while feeding the chickens. Then, he joined the conversation about cows over a glass of unfiltered sake. Every day, streams of smoke rose from the chimneys of houses in the village as they were cooking dinner. The village was filled with laughter, and everyone cheerfully greeted each other. As Tajima cows became a well-known and high-quality brand, people made reservations even before they went to the market. And above all, cow lovers got together like this at his place to discuss cows while enjoying their favorite sake.

Shusuke was living the happiest days of his life.

Chapter 12

Oyoshi and Violet

Since then, ten years had passed. The cow lovers still gathered at Shusuke's house to chat with fellow friends. For Oyoshi, Shusuke's happiness was her happiness; seeing him enjoying himself was the greatest joy for her. Those happy, joyful days motivated her to keep going forward.

Recently, however, she suffered from a dry cough and shortness of breath. Not only that, but also she sometimes coughed out pinkish frothy phlegm. Moreover, she had swelling in her legs and felt fatigued much more often than before. She kept believing that all of those symptoms were due to her age, but gradually it became harder and harder for her to even get out of bed.

However, it didn't catch Shusuke's attention, until one day, when he found Oyoshi in her bed unable to even get up to prepare breakfast. He was so startled that he immediately called a doctor. The doctor placed a tube-like instrument (Traube's Stethoscope) on her chest to examine her heart. A few moments later, Oyoshi spoke up.

"Doctor…my cough won't go away." She tried to lift herself.

The doctor removed the Traube's Stethoscope and told her, "No need to get up. Take a good rest. Eat something less salty, and you will get better. Maybe you can sleep better laying on your right side or in the Fowler's position."

As he advised her, he rolled up a blanket and placed it under her body.

"Shusuke, there's something I want to talk to you about later," the doctor told Shusuke, who had been anxiously watching them.

At the doctor's serious tone Shusuke swallowed hard. As he walked him to the door, the doctor turned around and spoke to Shusuke.

"Her heart is considerably weak, and her lungs have fluid retention. Her occasional coughing is not caused by a cold but by her heart. I observed the swelling in her feet, too. I'm sorry to say, but you should know that she doesn't have much time left. Take good care of her."

With the doctor's words, Shusuke panicked.

"But doc…, doctor. She has been fine and taking care of us until now. There is no way for her to suddenly get sick and die. It's impossible."

"Shusuke, she must have put up with the pain and pushed herself hard for a long time. She must have suffered from coughing since a while ago. By then, her lungs would have already filled up with fluid."

He knew about it. He knew she had been coughing or out of breath from time to time, but they laughed it off together, believing it was all because of her aging. No. He couldn't deny that he didn't want to admit the possibility of an illness, so he deliberately blamed it on aging.

Shusuke bit his lip with regret. Suddenly, what the town's express messenger had mentioned before struck his mind.

Shusuke returned to the bedroom and sat by Oyoshi.

"What did the doctor say?" she asked.

"He said that you've been working too hard. You need to take a rest. It's the same thing that he said earlier," said Shusuke, in a brusque manner. He honestly didn't know how to face her now.

"I know my body better than anyone else….I don't think I have much time left to live. I have one last place I want you to take me," she said.

"La… last place? What makes you say such nonsense? I can't live without you." Shusuke was   flustered.

Oyoshi smiled and sat up. "It's better for me to sit up like this to reduce the coughing. And you know…. you are such a terrible liar. I can tell that the doctor didn't tell you anything positive."

While she was talking to him, Shusuke couldn't look at her. He didn't know what to say to her at all.

"Honey, don't be so discouraged. You've gotten many cows that you've taken care of, so you won't be alone. You won't even have time to miss me. There will be plenty of things to do to keep you busy, right?"

Oyoshi reached out for him. Shusuke held her hand and sobbed. Somewhere far, the sound of mooing cows was heard. The cows, which rarely made any sounds, mooed calling Shusuke.

"You hear that? Your 'Shusuke vines' are calling you to get fed."

"Don't worry about the cows now. Where do you want to go?"

He had never raised his voice before, but this time, his tone of voice was strong.

Oyoshi answered, "That hill where you can see all the cows grazing in the village. It's where you told me about your dream to turn the Ojiro Valley into the world's best cattle ranch. Lately, I keep thinking about that day. Cough--- Cough…."

Shusuke rubbed her back. "Okay, that's enough, don't talk."

But she shook her head side to side and continued, "There, on that hill, at the base of the big cherry tree, there are a lot of small violets. They should be in bloom by now, so I want to see them, too."

"Violets? I don't remember seeing them on that hill."

"You can only see cows, can't you?"

The cows mooed again. Shusuke clicked his tongue and bit his lip.

"Until you became ill, I didn't realize how important you are in my life. Please forgive me. I've put you through a lot of trouble. I made you suffer like this…. I am such a fool."

He couldn't stop crying. He put a pillow under her body to lift her chest a little higher. He wiped his eyes, and he was about to head to check the cows. Right then, Sukezo came in.

"The cows asked me to get you, Shusuke."

His expression made Shusuke grin. "You finally began to understand what cows say, Sukezo."

Feeling embarrassed, Sukezo scratched his head.

When the two walked into the cowshed, Sukezo's assistant was carefully examining a cow from head to toe and also the hay. He seemed to have noticed that some herbs were missing from the feed blend.

"Oh, I see. I might have forgotten to mix Plantago and Chameleon plants in your feed. You really know your stuff, don't you?" He was talking to the cow.

"Believe it or not, she is quite precise about her feed. But when she refuses, gently tell her, 'you can't be picky, you need to eat everything,' and pet her on her shoulder blades like this. Then, she'll start eating."

When Shusuke began stroking the cow, she began to hungrily dig into the hay. As she ate, the aide added Plantago and other herbs into the feed.

"Wow, you are amazing, brother. My hat's off to you."

"You know, it's like the old proverb says, 'The ox knows his owner, but the people of Israel don't know. My people don't consider.' I have somewhere I need to go tomorrow morning, so will you check how much she eats for me?"

Shusuke returned to Oyoshi. She lay on her left side and was deep asleep. After watching her sleeping face for a while, he stood up to leave, but then she slightly opened her eyes.

"After taking a good rest, I feel much better now. Tomorrow morning, would you take me to the hill to look over the grazing cattle? I want to see the sunrise over the Ojiro valley."

"Don't push yourself. It's cold in the morning."

She slowly shook her head and insisted that she would be fine.

"Oh, well. I can't say no to you. I promise to take you there, so sleep tight tonight."

Oyoshi smiled happily and fell fast asleep.

The next morning, Shusuke fully stretched his back in his entrance under the still-dark sky.

Oyoshi turned around to reach for a makeup kit by the pillow, but trying to pull it in, she fell and coughed. Frothy, peach-colored sputum was coughed out into her hand. Startled by the sound, their young maid rushed over to help her. Oyoshi wiped the sputum away hurriedly with a piece of paper.

While holding up a candle, the maid helped Oyoshi sit up and asked, "Oh, my. What are you doing up so early in the morning?"

"I'm sorry to bother you, but could you hand me over......my makeup box...... and haori......? cough.... cough......."

The maid brought the box and the most beautiful haori for her. Oyoshi asked her to hold the candle while she put on makeup and the beautiful haori. When she was ready, she sat up on her bed waiting for Shusuke.

When Shusuke came to her bed, he found her sitting there smiling in the dim light of the fire. Her face was as pale as wax, but her red lipstick and rouge on her cheeks made her look slightly better.

"Oyoshi, are you all right? You are dressing up... You are so beautiful."

"Because I'm very excited. It's my first trip with you, so I'm ready to go." She made tiny fists to show him she would be fine.

"First trip...? We are going to the place we used to go while you were still healthy, so I'm not sure if we can call it a trip."

Shusuke carried her piggyback to the two-wheeled cart that he parked by the porch. He placed a backrest pillow and laid out cushions on the floor for her to sit up in the cart. Then, he covered her legs with another haori, untied the towel he had around his own neck to wrap it around her neck, and began to pull the big two-wheeled cart.

"Are you okay? If you don't feel good, just let me know. I'll take you back home right away,"

Shusuke turned around and reminded her.

Oyoshi smiled back. Along the way, she felt the breeze, the cool morning stillness, which made her happy. Not even in the slightest, was she afraid of death that might be soon approaching her. She had lived till today, and it didn't matter to her whether she would be taken to hell or heaven, now at this spot. Rather, she was silently giving huge applause for the life she lived until now.

As they approached the hill, the slowly rising sun began to color Oyoshi's cheeks orange. Shusuke used all the strength in his arms to keep the cart from rolling down the slope to show her the sky of the Ojiro village changing its color.

(That's right. Mozart's Clarinet Concerto No. 2 was played for this scene. Perhaps, Mozart composed this music as he had seen the scenery like Ojiro valley veiled in the morning haze.)

Little by little, the view in front of them was shifting its color from purple to red. Finally, the sun emerged from between the mountains.

"Oyoshi, the sun's rising!"

"Oh, yes. It's so beautiful......." She narrowed her eyes.

"We've feverishly come this far together, but sometimes it's nice to take a break, isn't it?"

"I agree......."

Shusuke truly felt the same way as well. And that realization made him regret not taking a moment to have such an experience with Oyoshi more often.

"Now, the cart can't go up beyond here, so I'm going to carry you up that hill on my back. Hang on tight."

Shusuke leaned the cart against a tree and carried Oyoshi on his back.

"Thank you, even though I must be heavy," said Oyoshi.

"You are lighter than the cows. You need to eat more; you are too light."

His habit of referring to everything in terms of cows, felt far and nostalgic to Oyoshi now.

"Yes, I'm sure I'll be able to eat a lot when I get home."

"Good. Keep it up, Oyoshi."

Through his back, his voice sounded reassuring.

"All right, now. We are at the hill. Can you see it, Oyoshi?"

"The cherry blossoms are already in full bloom before we noticed, aren't they? So beautiful."

In the morning glow, the sea of clouds on the mountain began to part. The night dewdrops lodged in the petals of the cherry blossoms began to shine all at once in the morning sun. From his back, Oyoshi looked up at them, slightly closing her eyes to the brightness, and felt great happiness. When the sea of clouds parted, the scene below was gradually revealed. Black cattle were already grazing. They could observe the cattle munching grass here and there. Smoke was rising out of the chimneys of the villagers' houses as they prepared their breakfasts.

Shusuke nodded broadly, looking up at the cherry trees. He turned to show her around.

"Look, over there, the cows are enjoying the grasses. Can you see them?"

"Yes, so many of them. Beautiful black cows. They're our children, aren't they? .... The children of 'Shusuke Vine.'"

"That's right. We have the best cattle farm that produces the best cattle in Japan. You've done a great job. Without you, this view would never exist. All the residents of this village can now provide their own food. You see, the smoke is rising as they cook their breakfasts. I am so happy. Without your support, this village would have been gone by now.

"Well, ... it's been a real pleasure ...... sharing a big dream with you..... ...I'm the luckiest ...... person in the world ...... and I've never felt ...... hardship... ...thank you ...... for everything..."

Rubbing her hands, Shusuke looked back at the roots of the tree, where violets were growing in clusters.

"Oyoshi, violets! There are so many violets blooming. Hold on one second."

Shusuke slowly bent down on his knees and picked a few violets. He slowly stood back up again and tried to put them in her left hand, which was wrapped around his shoulder. However, she did not try to grab them. Thinking that she could not see them, he let her fingers touch the violets. But her hand just dangled helplessly.

"Oyoshi? Oyoshi?"

Feeling uneasy, he called her name and shook her on his back. But no response returned from Oyoshi. Tears began to well up in his eyes as he carried the motionless Oyoshi on his back. Uncontrollable, overflowing tears kept falling. He could no longer see anything in the village.

Then, a gust of wind blew, fluttering the cherry blossom's petals away. Watching the petals soar high into the sky, tears welled up again in his eyes. He put the violets in her hand and held them for a while, but when he let go of her hand, the violets flew away from them together with the cherry petals lifting gently in the wind.

(For the ending, *Kyu Sakamoto's "The eyes of the heart (Kokoro no Hitomi)" began to play as an insert song with the original tune.)

Perhaps my emotions that had been smoldering over while watching the story were set off by this song. My chest filled up, and I could not breathe through my nose. Even long after the ending, I remained in my seat.

---

* Kyu Sakamoto: (1941-1985) Japanese Singer, internationally well known for his hit song "Sukiyaki."

Someone, who was once nobody, changed his village with his will. One person's dream attracted someone supporting his dream, and little by little, the circle of support began to expand, and eventually, his dream even became the dream of the entire village. That's right. A person with a dream. The people who understand his dream. The supporters around him. There are people in each position. It's like baseball or soccer as well. If any of these people don't exist, it is not possible to make his dream come true.

Do I really want to pursue my career as a cook throughout my entire life? Have I been doing it with enough joy to make it my mission to serve delicious food to customers? There are probably plenty of cooks in this world who are as good as me. Even if I don't cook, someone else will. Furthermore, I came to Japan to learn how to cook steak that can bring out the flavor of the meat itself, but it has already become a well-known cooking method in Japan. So importantly, I want to pass on the "passion for life" shown in this film to those who live with difficulty. I want to help them realize that anyone with a dream has this much power.

The Final Chapter

After returning to the kitchen, Chef Maeda and I looked over the tables left in the quiet hall, from the food delivery window. I noticed a small sake bottle on the table, which had a painting of violet flowers. It made me feel as if I were in a movie.

As the chef slowly walked out of the kitchen, the soft orange light shining through the window enveloped him. He slowly took off his white hat, placed it on his chest, and bowed his head to the empty hall. I watched the scene from a little behind. I gave a round of applause to a man who had achieved success in the world of Japanese cuisine......well, that's how I remember......, but I am not sure whether I was dreaming within my dream or in an even deeper dream.

Now, I am in a lecture hall. Students are rushing to the podium applauding, and soon, I am surrounded by them. The film that I ran for my students had ended. If these young students were moved by the story like this and grasped the essence of it, then it was a success. I have found a way of life that satisfies me, and here I am.

Thirty years have passed since Shusuke Maeda's death. Farm cattle have been replaced by tractors, and Tajima cattle have gradually become more valuable as meat cattle. In an attempt to improve their size, they were crossbred with foreign breeds, but they became too large to work in the narrow terraced rice fields, and their violent temper was not suitable for farming. Crossbreeding Tajima cattle with other local cattle from each region did not work out well either. It did not produce good cattle. Most of them became mongrels, which caused the price of cattle to continue to drop.

Later, Matsuzo Tajiri of Ojiro Village completely fell for a cow passing on the road and sold his family fortune to buy it. It turned out, that it was a descendant of the Shusuke-vine, "Atsuta-vine," named Fukue-go.

Fukue-go continued to produce excellent female cows that looked just like her every year, and seven years later, a male cow, Tajiri-go, was born. The prefectural government purchased Tajiri-go to research the genes with veterinarian Yoshio Matsumura. After years of research, they succeeded in the homogenization of the genes of Tajiri-go, which had strong and good genes. Today, 99% of Japan's brand beef cattle are descendants of this Tajiri breed.

-The end-

About Shusuke Maeda (1797-1872)

Born in Mizuma Ojiroku Kami-cho, Mikata District, Hyogo, he devoted his life to improving the Tajima beef strain and eventually succeeded in establishing "Shusuke Tsuru," a lineage named after Shusuke. "Shusuke Tsuru" was the basis of today's "Tajima Beef" lineage. (From Encyclopedia of Tajima URL: https://www.tanshin-kikin.jp/)

About Tajima Beef

Tajima beef, also called Japanese Black, is a cattle breed produced in Hyogo Prefecture. Tajima beef is the root of Japanese brand beef. Kobe beef, Matsuzaka beef, and Omi beef are well-known beef brands which are famous worldwide, yet there is no such breed as Kobe or Matsuzaka. The actual breed of those cattle is Tajima cattle, which is the root of those brand beef cattle. Once they reach a certain age (about 9 months old), Tajima calves are put up for auction and sent to each region where they will be carefully raised and fattened by the local farmers. Those locally produced, highest quality Tajima cattle have earned a high reputation as branded beef. (JA Tajima URL: https://www.ja-tajima.or.jp/)

Author's Profile

Yoshiko Kagawa (Formerly known as Yoshiko Matsumoto)

Born in Tokushima prefecture, Japan. A physician in internal medicine and a writer.

A member of Tokushima Minami Rotary Club.

A member of The Japan P.E.N. club.

A director of NPO, "Approach for Life Saving."

In 1993, Opened Bunkei Memorial Internal Medicine Clinic

In 2005, Opened an elderly care group home, "Hawaii"

Other contributions including:

In charge of General Affairs at the main office of FC Kyoiku.com "Tanoshii Sakai-shiki Kaiga Kyoshitsu" Main Office (President: Shingo Sakai, Representative: Maine Kagawa)

Introduction of Suzuki Method of Talent Education Research Institute (The Headquarters are located in Matsumoto City, Nagano Prefecture, President: Koji Toyota) to Tokushima Prefecture

Major Works:

1999-2001
Published a series of articles in the monthly magazine "Kyoshitsu Two Way" (Meijitosho Shuppan)

2004-2006
Published a series of articles in the monthly magazine "Katei Kyoiku Two Way" (Meijitosho Shuppan)

2004
"Tadaima Yume Shinryoshitsu ha Daihanjyo" (Shinpusha)

2005
Bestseller: "Do You Know The Ave Maria Violin?" Japanese Ver. (Shinpusha)

Selected as one of the assigned books for the 2014 National Book Report Contest for high school students. Published in paperback as well.

2006
Script Writing for Radio Drama "Oto no Kanatani"

2016
Bestseller : "Awa Story Starts from Japan" (Publisher: Hikaru Land)

2021
"Do You Know The Ave Maria Violin?" Published in English
(Babel Press U.S.A)

2022
"Asuka: The Karate Girl: Asuka and Origami Giraffe" Published in English
(Babel Press U.S.A)

Reference

Interview with Mr. Toshiie Maeda

Interview with Mr. Noboru Tajiri

Gyusho Ueda, K.K. Ueda Chikusan field work

Tajima Plateau Botanical Gardens, K.K. Muraoka Shinko Public Corporation

Interview and fieldwork with Mr. Akihito Tamaru

Other   Historical documents of Tajima cattle

Seirangama   Yusuke Matsushita, Toshiyuki Matsushita, Field work

"Kokoro no Hitomi" Song by Kyu Sakamoto Lyric by Toyohisa Araki

Composed by Takashi Miki

"I Have a Dream" Speech by Martin Luther King Jr.

www.ingramcontent.com/pod-product-compliance
Lightning Source LLC
Chambersburg PA
CBHW070640130626
46555CB00006B/2636